MELTING POINT

MELTING POINT

POINT

THE MOONLIGHT SOCIETY

OCTAVIA CLARKE *and* FENN COPPER

First published in Great Britain
Copyright © 2022 Octavia Clarke and Fenn Copper.
All rights reserved

This paperback edition 2022
1

ISBN: 979-8357290113

Dedication

With thanks and gratitude to our friends and family
for their encouragement and support.

Chapter 1 – The Accidental Diamond

Shearcourt Demesne, Donegal, Ireland, March 2022

The soft morning sunlight streamed in through the elegant sash windows of the study.

William turned the page and flattened the pink paper of the *Financial Times* on his desk.

He poured a fresh cup of tea, fragrant steam sending wisps of bergamot into the air, and settled down to read. The finance minister for the United Arab Emirates (UAE) hailed the imposition of increased scrutiny of gold smuggling into Dubai a year ago as a success. Measures including introducing a ban on carrying gold in hand luggage had crippled traditional smuggling routes, reducing the flow of illegally mined gold from Africa to Dubai and then on to other countries, with its origins blurred and a gloss of legitimacy acquired.

He ran his finger over the raised pattern of his cup, deep in thought. The Moonlight Society had been watching activities in Dubai for some time, intervening where it could. It was an easy route for smugglers because, much as they denied it, the authorities exercised much less vigour in checking certificates for gold entering the country than any European nation. Consequently, gold mined in illegal, polluting, exploitative mines in Africa had run through Dubai in a steady trickle. If that leak had been stemmed, where was that gold going now?

His phone vibrated. Unknown caller. He raised an eyebrow but tapped the screen and accepted the call.

"William speaking."

"William, how are you? Still on that weirdly named boat of yours?"

William smiled at the familiar, lightly German-inflected voice of Jurgen.

"Jurgen. You know the *Accidental Diamond* is a yacht."

"It's little more than a leaky dinghy. I don't know why you keep it."

"You're right. The salon is scarcely more impressive than an airport lounge, and the master stateroom is barely big enough for a four-poster bed."

"I'm just offended you haven't invited me for a holiday on her." Jurgen gave an exaggerated sigh.

William chuckled. "I wish I could, but it'd be rather a giveaway. We'll have to wait until you've retired from Interpol."

"Something to look forward to. The daily running costs of that thing are probably more than my annual pension will be. I'd love to buy a boat, but those things are expensive."

"Well, you know what they say, Jurgen, there's rich, and there's boat rich."

"Shouldn't that be yacht rich?"

"No, yacht rich is a different category altogether… and as it happens, I'm not on the Diamond at the moment. I'm at Shearcourt."

"Ah, that other place you haven't invited me to! Anyway, enough pleasantries. I wondered what your take is on the Dubai gold-smuggling situation."

"There was me thinking this was a social call." William sat back in his chair, tracing the grain of the wood with his finger.

"Maybe when I've retired."

"Dubai has been playing on my mind. That gold has to be going somewhere. There will be a gap in the market for new smuggling routes, but I can't see how the cartels will find a route as low effort and easy as the Dubai one. All you need is a willing idiot with some hand luggage."

"There isn't one. It's as simple as that. Which means someone, somewhere, will be trying to test out security gaps across the travel and import/export industries to find the next best option."

"I'll keep my ear to the ground."

"I was hoping you'd do something a little more proactive than that, William."

William raised an eyebrow. "Is that a formal request for the assistance from the Moonlight Society?"

"It is. And we will, of course, as always, deny all knowledge of the Society, if your investigations are indelicate enough to attract attention."

"We wouldn't have it any other way."

"We think there has to be some higher-level corruption within transport, travel and manufacturing for a new route to work well, so that's where we'd like your help. The sort of people likely to be involved in that level of operation are rather out of our sphere of influence – you know, those boat-rich guys."

"That'd definitely be the yacht-rich guys."

"Whatever. Your men with more money than sense."

"Can't argue with that. We'll see what we can do."

"Thanks, William."

William put the phone down on his desk and leaned back in his chair. All signs pointed towards increased illegal gold mining production in Africa, not decreased production, despite the Dubai crackdown. That meant someone had got organised. And that meant significant corruption.

William sat back and looked out across the gardens. The lavender had not yet begun to bloom, but cheerful spring colours filled the flower beds beyond the sweeping stone steps down to the lawns. Dark clouds casting shadows over Classiebawn Castle and the mountains beyond the edges of his land promised an afternoon of the frequent rain that kept the trees and grasses their fresh, intense green. The air drifting through the open windows held the sharp, clean iodine tang of sea and seaweed from Donegal Bay. On the lawn, his two Great Dane and Weimaraner cross dogs napped on a sunny patch of grass. It was so peaceful here, but there was work to be done that would take him back out into the world soon enough. He opened his contact list and dialled.

"Hello, Ian speaking."

"Tin Belly, how are you?" William said with a smile.

"Ha ha, William! I'm fine. You caught me between endless meetings. Jenny is holding off my calls so I can finally eat my damn sandwiches. How are you?"

"I'm well, at home in Shearcourt at the minute. I have some beautiful horses here if you want to come over with Shona and the girls in the summer."

"The breeding programme is going well, then, I take it."

"Yes, and John does an admirable job of training them. We'll have some champion jumpers from our stable yet." William looked fondly at the framed photos of horses that lined the walls.

"I'd love to come over. I'll speak to Shona about dates."

"Good, please do. It'd be lovely to see you."

"And you. But you didn't call to invite me to Shearcourt. What can I help you with?"

"I need a favour." William smiled at the brief silence at the other end of the line.

"Well, I do owe you one. Go on, what is it and how much work will it create for me?"

"Hopefully, not that much work for you; I need to borrow some of your manpower."

"You do know that we've got a critical shortage of prison officers right now?"

"That's because you don't pay them as well as we do in Northern Ireland."

6

"Yeah, they get danger money over in Northern Ireland, though."

"It's not prison officer support I need. I need to borrow one of your counter-corruption experts. Someone with good insights into behaviour, organisational and individual psychology and corruption. Someone capable, flexible and able to operate with the utmost discretion."

"How long do you need them for?"

"Three months."

"Would you like the blood of my firstborn child whilst you are at it?"

William smothered a laugh. "If I recall, I'm Ada's godfather, so no."

He heard Ian tap his fingers thoughtfully against the phone.

"OK. I have someone in mind. Grace Adair – she's operated some high-level corruption and fraud investigations across establishments in the region, and frankly, I like her. She's sharp, hardworking, and pragmatic. You're not allowed to steal her, though, William. I need her back after her three months are up. I'll have to pull some serious strings to get her boss on board – and then there's the question of whether Grace will agree. What level of backing do you have for this project?"

"Jurgen cleared it."

"Right. That'll do. Am I allowed to ask what the assignment is?"

"It's probably better you don't know. And work out a cover story for where Miss Adair will be whilst on assignment with me."

"Right…" Ian drummed his fingers on the desk as he went through possible options, "we could say the Falklands prison service are struggling with corruption issues at the moment, so we're sending her over there to head up their task force. As far as I'm aware, no one at my prison has connections with the staff there, so it's unlikely anyone will figure out that she's not there."

"That works."

"How soon do you need her?"

"Wednesday?"

"Jesus, William!"

"I'm sure by the time you've made a couple of calls, you'll have it all in hand."

"I'm never going to get to eat these sandwiches, am I? At least she already travels around the country frequently and often at short notice as part of her role. I don't know much about her circumstances beyond that."

William heard the sound of a Tupperware lid snap irritably back on a tub.

"I'll make it up to you with a dinner of salmon that we'll catch with our own hands when you come over. The Society will offer Miss Adair every assistance to enable her to fulfil the assignment."

"I'll hold you to that and to the dinner. Make sure you don't break my staff member, William. I want her back in one piece."

"Of course. I'll come over tomorrow to meet her."

"I have time at one o'clock."

"See you then."

William ended the call and sat looking out at the gentle green landscape before him. Tomorrow, he'd need to be in the grey, claustrophobic crush of London once again.

***

Grace wiggled her toes vigorously in her low-heeled loafers under the conference table, trying to focus on the movement to keep her awake. Angus, the head of regional security, was droning on and on about the new counter-corruption training package implementation plan.

Grace had little interest in this. She wrote the package. The nuances of staff rotas, shutdown days and meeting rooms were not her concern, and much as she appreciated Angus's attention to detail and the complexity of his role, she'd been in this damn meeting for three hours already. No one had eaten lunch. The coffee urn was empty. Grace wondered how she had come to feel so bored by her job. She'd worked hard to rise through the ranks in the psychology division before moving over to the counter-corruption team. It had seemed like a dream role, and in many ways, it was, but the meetings, bureaucracy and red tape consumed the joy and rewards of her work now, leaving Grace feeling flat and dissatisfied most of the time.

"Over to you, Grace," Angus said.

Finally, Grace thought, pulling up her slides on the large screen over the conference table.

"Our main focus on a national level has been implementing policy and practice to disrupt opportunities for corruption within our systems. Increased accountability checks and attention to corruption risk factors in systems and processes are part of the solution. In-depth investigations and root cause analysis work, have helped to break up several large-scale corruption operations across the country. We've been able to identify areas in need of development to prevent future corruption and to deter staff from engaging in corrupt behaviours. However, this activity, though important, does not address the role of the individual in corruption and the disruption of corruption. Our newly updated training package aims to meet this need. When we have staff who are poorly paid, in a society where the cost of living is rapidly escalating, the risk of them feeling increased financial pressures and becoming vulnerable to corrupt practices is magnified."

There were uncomfortable looks around the table. The gradual erosion of staff pay and conditions was a sore point. It had contributed to catastrophic staff retention and recruitment issues, in addition to having a crucial role to play in the problems of staff corruption across the whole prison system. Grace looked around. Only Mark, the Prison Officers' Association union rep looked her in the eye. He beamed and gave her a not very discreet nod and a wink.

"Our new package aims to support staff to identify their individual responsibilities in identifying corruption risks – including noticing when they may have become compromised and understanding the consequences of corruption in terms of the safety and fidelity of the system – but also aims to empower staff to seek support if they are struggling. We have, in partnership with the unions, worked hard to ensure staff feel supported to access financial advice and personal support. A well-supported, well-informed, healthy workforce is less at risk of engaging in corruption and–"

Grace broke off as the phone rang.

Angus reached over and pressed a button. "Angus speaking."

Jenny, the governor's secretary, spoke. "Hi Angus, the number one said that he requires Grace's presence in his office. Can you send her down?"

Angus frowned at Grace, who shrugged, but picked up her papers and made her excuses.

Relief surged through her at the opportunity to leave the near-endless meeting, but also a twinge of apprehension. Being called to the governor's office like this was highly unusual.

Her footsteps echoed as she strode through the long corridors, unlocking and locking half a dozen gates on the short trip from the security office to the other side of the admin block, chain jingling on her belt as she returned her keys to their pouch.

Grace smoothed her austere black blazer and ran a hand over her tightly braided hair as she approached the final gate before the governor's suite.

Jenny's desk faced the door, with her office serving as a waiting room for the governor's office behind her.

She looked up at Grace with a wry smile. "That was quick. I thought it might take you a little longer to make your excuses from Angus's meeting."

"I wouldn't want to keep the number one waiting," Grace said with a grin.

"Go on in. They're waiting for you."

"They?"

"They," Jenny confirmed.

Grace waited a moment to see if she would add more, then gave up. Jenny wasn't going to elaborate. She knocked on the door and pushed it open as a hearty command to enter rang out.

The governor was sitting at his desk. A tall man sat in one of the pair of leather armchairs that faced him. They both rose to greet her.

"Grace, this is William Anderson."

Grace took the offered hand. His fingers were warm, and although he had neatly filed nails, Grace felt slight callouses on the underside of his fingers as he lightly pressed hers. His face was handsome – rugged and slightly sun-kissed. His suit was impeccable, but she could almost smell the fresh air from him. This was a man who liked to be out of doors, she thought.

"Pleased to meet you, Mr Anderson," Grace said, falling back on formality, unsure of the nature of this meeting.

"William, please. Ian and I were in the military together before our paths took us in different directions."

It was widely known around the prison that he was an ex-military man, like many of the older prison officers, although she couldn't recall anyone mentioning his regiment. She glanced down. His tie clip had a tiny eagle and a motto – "*Honi soit qui mal y pense*." Grace searched her memory. Her elderly neighbour when she was a child had been an ardent military historian, and she'd spent many hours looking through his books and memorabilia with him. The household cavalry, perhaps. She looked discreetly at the photos on the shelves behind his desk. Ian's wife and children, a rugby team photo, dogs – and a horse. Yes, household cavalry would make sense.

The governor smiled warmly. "William is a close friend, and I have had cause to use his excellent professional knowledge several times over the years, meaning that I owe him several favours. One of which I'm hoping, Grace, you'll help me discharge."

William pulled out the leather chair next to him and gestured for her to take a seat. She sat down and looked curiously from one to the other.

"What's the favour?"

Ian glanced at William and nodded.

"Ian is willing to release you for a period of three months, with your consent. It would be a secondment of sorts to provide consultancy around corruption as part of an ongoing project of international importance. It would require some travel, fully funded, of course."

"Has my line manager cleared this?" Grace asked, incredulous at the possibility. She was midway through several major internal investigations and training projects.

"She has," Ian confirmed. "This instruction comes from the highest authority and with the highest level of secrecy. As far as everyone else is concerned, you'll have been seconded to the Falklands prison service to offer them support with an urgent project there."

Grace sat back in her chair. This was unreal. "If I agree to it, when would this secondment start?" she asked.

"Tomorrow."

Grace sat back in her chair, eyes on the ground, deep in thought. There was a long silence before she lifted her eyes to William's.

"OK."

"Pack a case with clothes suitable for a warm climate, some formal and evening wear and a jacket for cooler evenings. If any more specific items of clothing are necessary, these will be provided. A car will collect you at 10 a.m."

"What do I tell my family?"

"That you're on secondment in the Falklands," Ian said with a wink.

"Do I get a choice about this?"

"Of course," William said, his face serious. "And any assistance you require to manage your personal affairs will be provided whilst you are away."

Grace thought for a moment. "OK. But if I'm packing for a warm climate, we might need to rethink the Falklands story. My knowledge of the Falklands is limited, but I don't believe it's that warm there at this time of year, or in fact, at any time of year. If I come home with a tan, that rather calls the cover story into question."

"Good point. We'll add a week's leave for a holiday at the end of your secondment, how about that?" Ian said.

"We have access to a residence you can spend your leave at if you wish to," William added.

Grace shook her head in disbelief. She thought about the endless meetings that filled her schedule for the next few weeks. Or had filled her schedule. Her heart lifted at the thought of not having to pinch herself to stay awake whilst she listened to Angus's lengthy, earnest presentations.

"If I'm not going to the Falklands, where am I going?"

"We'll start in the Mediterranean. The operational details are sensitive and will be disclosed once you arrive at our secure base," William said.

"Well, this is all very unexpected. Do you mind if I head home? I have packing to do."

"Of course. Thank you, Grace," Ian said.

William stood and again offered his hand. "I'll brief you on arrival tomorrow; I look forward to working with you."

Grace shook his hand and nodded to the governor. She closed the office door and took a deep breath.

"Enjoy the Falklands," Jenny said, not looking up from her computer.

***

The interior of the club in Belgravia was dim. Leather armchairs clustered around mahogany tables. Firelight flickered on bookcases filled with handsomely bound books.

William smiled. This place was a relic of a bygone age, but it was one of the only places in London where he felt truly at ease.

Stephen and Ian had taken a table by the fire. William's heart warmed at the sight of his old friends. He regretted that Thomas Campbell, their commanding officer, wasn't with them. It'd been a long time since they'd seen him and he missed Campbell's brisk, rough presence. A whiskey was waiting for William – no ice, no water. He shook hands with them and picked up his drink as he sat down, swirling the amber liquid in the glass and taking a sniff. The smell of an orchard in autumn, with a hint of roasted hazelnut.

"Irish?" he asked Stephen.

"Of course."

William took a sip. The rich fruitiness was deepened by the warmth of oak and a tang of sea salt.

"Single malt. Twenty-four-year-old?"

"No."

"Twenty-eight?"

"No."

William whistled softly. "Thirty?"

"Yes."

"Teeling?"

"Yes!"

"Ah, the vintage reserve?"

"1991."

"Pricey."

Stephen smiled. "Seven hundred pounds. It's on the Society's tab."

William laughed. "My turn to pick next – and you both know the penalty if you don't guess."

They'd played this game as long as they'd known each other. Even in Afghanistan, when they'd had to source dubious-quality whiskey and sneak it past their senior officers.

Ian smiled, holding his glass up to catch the light of the fire.

"Do you remember when we got so drunk that we fell asleep in the kitchens when we tried to make toast at 3 a.m.?"

Stephen laughed. "Yeah, and I remember we had a 2K run around the compound at 6 a.m. the next morning."

William winced. "I threw up in every other ditch for the first kilometre, trying desperately not to let Campbell see me."

"And when we got back, he made us clean out every single bog," Ian added.

Stephen groaned. "God, the smell in that heat! Campbell always found a way to let us know that he knew what we'd been up to without calling us out on it."

"They were the pits," Ian said. "Literally the pits, given that we had no plumbing."

William raised his glass. "To Campbell – it is in defiance of him that we drink whiskey today."

They raised their whiskeys in a toast. "To Campbell."

"Have you seen him lately?" William asked, turning to Ian.

"Not for a while. Shona keeps in touch with his wife, and we keep meaning to go over to visit, but you know how it is with the kids."

"You owe us a visit, too," Stephen said. "I've got some nice little ponies that your girls would love."

Ian sighed. "I know, and William has promised me some fishing. As soon as things quieten down at the prison, we'll get some dates together."

Stephen smiled, shaking his head. "When did life get so complicated for us all?"

"Complicated?" Ian raised his eyebrows. "Nowadays, you and William are off gallivanting around the world on a yacht the size of Norwich half the time when you're not doing whatever it is you do that we don't talk about the rest of the time. You should try co-ordinating ballet classes, gymnastics, music lessons for three girls and attending Parents' Association meetings that require a level of diplomacy usually seen at international nuclear armament talks. That's complicated."

William laughed. "Shona and the girls are your world. Don't even try to pretend otherwise."

Ian rolled his eyes. "Of course they are, although my example of domestic bliss doesn't seem to have been enough to convince you two to settle down."

Stephen shrugged. "Well, I have someone in my life. On the other hand, William doesn't show any signs of letting go of his bachelor status."

William chuckled. "Cora?"

"Yep," Stephen replied happily.

William raised his glass and tipped it towards Stephen. "I noticed how you look at each other when I've seen you over at the stables. Good choice."

He stored that fact away for future reference. Stephen spent a lot of time away from Ireland, so they might need to reconsider his workload in future. He felt a tug of loneliness in his gut. He missed Sadie.

Stephen caught his eye. "What's happening at the prison, Ian?" he said, changing the conversation.

"Staffing problems. We can't keep staff – the older staff are retiring as soon as possible. The younger staff come in on poorer pay and conditions, and we can't keep hold of them. Additionally, the corruption issues are increasing because of the lack of stability," Ian said, his voice heavy.

"In that case, I appreciate you lending us your counter-corruption lead," William said.

"Lending is the word, William. You can't keep her." Ian shook his finger at him.

William held up his empty glass. "I believe it's your turn to choose our whiskey."

Ian narrowed his eyes. "Don't think I didn't notice that evasion. It's lucky for you that I like whiskey too much to argue."

Chapter 2 – Debts of Honour

The air felt gritty in the city. It was too far from the coast for any breeze and the dense city smog sat heavily on the horizon, like morning mist on the crest of a mountain.

Francesco sat down on the warm pavement. Although it was still early, the summer sun was already beating down on the street outside the factory, and the rough concrete warmed the bare skin of his calves as he waited, scanning the faces queuing up to start their shift, looking for his father.

He wasn't there. Francesco sighed. The shift started in a quarter of an hour, so there was still time. He rolled a shell between his fingers, feeling the familiar ridges and contours. He'd never seen the sea, but he'd traded one of his friends the shell for a handful of marbles he'd reclaimed from the periphery of the school playground. He held it to his ear, hearing the roar his friend had told him was the trapped noise of ocean waves.

Francesco looked up, the shell still held to his ear. A tall, slender man with kind eyes was watching him from the queue. Francesco looked down at his shoes, rubbing at the dust that sneaked into the cracked leather, no matter how many times he cleaned them.

"Back again?"

Francesco jumped. The man had left the queue and gazed down at him, smiling gently.

Francesco nodded.

"I see you here waiting most mornings. Who are you waiting for?"

"My papa."

"Who is your papa?"

"Antonio Castelli."

"Ah."

The man dropped into a crouch. Francesco cautiously looked him in the eye.

"Why do you wait for him?"

"Because he doesn't come home much, and then me and Mama don't have food. Mama can't work since she hurt her back."

"I see. Shouldn't you be on your way to school right now?"

Francesco shrugged. "I can't leave Mama with no food."

The man stood up. Francesco looked down at the shell and turned it over and over in his small fingers.

"Here." The man handed Francesco a paper bag. The clean scent of fresh bread rose from it. "My wife gave me this to have with my coffee, but I'm not hungry this morning."

Francesco took the bag. "Thank you, sir." His mouth watered at the smell of the bread.

"No problem. Give everything in that bag to your mama and then go on to school now, OK?"

"OK."

The tall man turned away.

"Wait!" Francesco called out.

The man turned back and looked down at Francesco.

"What's your name, sir?"

"Fausto Rossi," the man said, smiling.

"I'll pay you back for the bread, Mr Rossi."

Francesco's expression was serious. Mr Rossi examined his face. The boy looked determined; his chin lifted proudly.

"OK, young man. You can buy me breakfast one day when you're a little older."

Francesco nodded. He stood up, holding the warm, fragrant bag to his chest, and began to walk home.

Once he'd rounded the corner, he opened the bag and peeped at the bread rolls, hunger gnawing at his stomach. Nestled next to the greaseproof paper wrapping were a few creased bank notes. Francesco turned and ran back to the factory. The long line of men had vanished through the tall doors.

Chapter 3 – The Briefing

Grace sat on her bed, looking at the clothes scattered around her.

Her stomach rumbled. She looked at her watch. 8 p.m. After leaving the governor's office, she'd driven home, feeling a little dazed, and pulled her dusty suitcase down from the attic.

Several hours spent trying to put together a suitable collection of clothing had left her feeling exasperated. She had work clothes – suits appropriate for cold London weather in a Victorian prison with poor heating, with one linen suit for the summer and some lighter trousers and tops for the rare days when the prison made the leap from chilled gloom to sweltering heat. She had holiday clothes, which had gone unworn for the last two years. These mainly consisted of light dresses and shorts.

"Bring evening wear," Grace muttered to herself, rolling her eyes.

This would do. She pulled out a navy silk shirt dress. Reaching deep into the back of her closet, she found two other formal dresses, relics of past stints as a wedding guest.

Grace walked over to her bookcase, pulled out half a dozen novels and tucked them into the top pocket of her case. She looked at her academic books and frowned. With no idea what the assignment was about, it was hard to know what might be useful. She picked out several books on organisational psychology, corruption and risk assessment, then added her Kindle to the top of the pile.

Anything else she needed, William could reimburse her for downloading – assuming they'd have the internet at this mystery sunshine location.

Grace raided her desk for a handful of her favourite black pens and a couple of notebooks.

She looked around her apartment and suddenly panicked. Would the place be OK without anyone to take care of it? Ground-floor flats could be vulnerable to break-ins. Grace made a brief survey of each room, guiltily noticing her already slightly neglected houseplants.

Her phone buzzed in her pocket and she pulled it out. A text message from a number she did not recognise.

"Miss Adair, I neglected to mention that you will have full access to our concierge service. If you leave your keys with the driver tomorrow, he will ensure that your home is well looked-after and secure. You may leave him a list of tasks you would like attending to in your absence. Regards, W."

"Our?" Grace thought. Who did William Anderson work for? The organisation stood above the prison service and had access to high-level governmental lines of clearance. MI5? MI6?

She looked at her plants. "It sounds like you will get better looked-after than if I was at home."

***

Grace's alarm broke into her dreams, jolting her awake. She reached over and silenced the beeping. Her eyes felt gritty. She'd fallen into bed following a long shower late last night. After sending emails to her manager and team about outstanding tasks that would need covering in her absence, she'd called her mother. The conversation with her mother had been stressful. She, understandably, found it hard to grasp how and why a sudden, urgent assignment was taking her daughter to the Falklands, of all places. Grace felt a pang of guilt for lying to her when she checked her inbox and saw that her mother had emailed her half a dozen articles about penguins, Falklands wildlife and the best places to photograph penguins in the early hours of the morning. Penguins seemed to figure quite highly in possible leisure activities in the Falklands, in her mother's estimation.

Then had come a difficult conversation with Dave. Dave was nice. Thoughtful, kind, reliable. He had an excellent job at a big accounting firm. His family were nice – they played board games together after Christmas dinner. Grace and Dave had dated on and off for the last couple of years, but she did not really want to settle down with him. He listened patiently when she talked about books she loved or when her imagination drew her mind off down some fanciful rabbit hole, but he didn't really understand her. It made her feel that she had to dim her light around him – which made her feel guilty because she knew he didn't mean to make her feel like that. Going away for three months provided an opportunity to make a clean break. Dave had been incredulous that she was going away so suddenly, then sad, in an understanding way, and had told her that he'd be waiting for her. She had asked him not to, but he'd insisted he'd be there when she came back.

Grace stretched, staying under the duvet, holding on to the warmth of the night and the familiarity of her bed for a little longer.

She replayed the meeting with William Anderson in her head. He was tall – handsome in a granite-hewn kind of way. His voice was refined and smooth and held the trace of an accent – Scottish? Irish? The number one had mentioned that he had been in the military with Anderson. Although his immaculately cut suit suggested a man of business, his broad shoulders and well-muscled frame carried an air of athleticism and strength.

What favour might the governor owe this clearly wealthy, powerful man? A vague red flag waved at the edges of Grace's mind – she was a counter-corruption lead, after all – but her boss' rapid agreement suggested this was a high-level, formal assignment which must have received central clearance.

Who was this man?

Grace got up. She turned her duvet back to air and smoothed her pillows. It was odd to think she wouldn't be sleeping in her own bed for weeks to come, when only yesterday morning she'd arisen confident in the knowledge that the coming months would see each morning starting the same, over and over again.

She showered, dressed, ate a hasty breakfast, supplemented by two cups of coffee, and made the final checks of her luggage.

A light tap sounded at the door. Grace glanced out of the window. A silver Range Rover was parked outside her house. She couldn't see if there was anyone in the back of the car as the windows were tinted a discreet grey that matched the tone of the bodywork.

Grace pulled on her coat and opened the door.

"Good morning, Miss Adair."

The driver was tall, heavy-set and had a battered face with surprisingly long-lashed bright blue eyes.

Grace looked up at him, feeling small. He must be at least six-foot eight, towering over her slim five-foot-four frame.

"Good morning, Mr…?"

"Stephen. You can call me Stephen." His voice was gravelly and heavy with a Glasgow accent.

"Good morning, Stephen. You can call me Grace."

"Thank you, Miss Adair," Stephen said with a crooked grin.

Grace shrugged and smiled. In prison, everyone called you Miss, so it felt rather familiar, but for all she knew, Stephen had instructions to refer to her as Miss Adair.

She stepped aside, and he walked into the house to start loading her luggage into the car.

Grace shut the door and applied the deadlock.

"Do you have a list of instructions for me to pass to the concierge?" Stephen asked.

Grace took an envelope from her pocket and added her keys to it.

"Yes, thanks, Stephen. Will someone be able to keep an eye on my car, too?"

"Of course. Are your car keys in the envelope?"

"Yes, along with my registration number."

"Excellent. We'll ensure your car is taken care of. It'll be washed and serviced, ready for your return."

"Thank you."

Nervousness fluttered in her stomach as she handed him the little package. She took a deep breath and walked over to the car, where Stephen offered his hand to help her in. Grace took it, her fingers cold against his big, rough hand, and stepped into the car.

This, she thought, was going to be an unusual few months at work.

"Where are we headed, Stephen?"

"London City Airport, Miss Adair. Then on to meet Mr Anderson in Gibraltar."

"Gibraltar! Ah, to HMP Windmill?"

"No, not to the prison. We're going to join Mr Anderson on his yacht. Gibraltar was the most convenient port for the *Accidental Diamond* to pick you both up."

"His yacht! I've never been on a yacht. How big is it?"

"In the top one per cent."

"Jesus," Grace muttered, then, collecting herself, added, "the *Accidental Diamond*… that's an unusual name."

"Named after a horse."

"Unusual name for a horse, too."

"I'm sure Mr Anderson will tell you the story himself at some point."

"I'll add it to the ever-increasing list of questions I have for him," Grace said dryly.

Stephen glanced at her in the rear-view mirror. "Short notice assignment?"

"Yep."

"The Society often needs specialist personnel at short notice."

"The Society?"

"Something else that Mr Anderson will tell you about."

"I see. Have you worked for the Society for long?"

"Since I left my regiment."

"You're ex-military too, then?"

"A lot of us are. Most of Mr Anderson's immediate staff served under him."

"What regiment?"

"The Blues and Royals."

Grace nodded. The Blues and Royals were one of the London regiments attached to the Household Cavalry.

"I guess that explains why the yacht is named after a horse."

"Mr Anderson is fond of horses."

"Do you ride?"

"When I can."

"If you don't mind me saying, you're quite a tall man. You must need quite a tall horse."

Stephen laughed. "It's not always easy to find a horse, but Mr Anderson's stable has quite a number of horses of around seventeen hands, so when we're at his house, I can ride whenever I wish."

"Where is his house?"

"Donegal in Ireland, but he grew up in Northern Ireland."

"Ah." Grace nodded. She hadn't been able to pinpoint his accent, but the cadences of Northern Ireland, softened by travel and time away from home perhaps, were there.

They drove on in companionable silence for a while. Grace liked the big man. He had a reassuring air of solid trustworthiness.

The car pulled into the entrance to the airport but headed away from the long-stay car park that Grace usually used.

"Are you just dropping me off, Stephen?"

"No, I'll fly with you, but we're headed to the jet centre."

"What's that?"

"The part of the airport that private aircraft passengers use."

"Oh. So, we're not flying with Ryanair, then?"

"No, Miss Adair."

Stephen parked in a sleek, secure parking facility and shepherded them through check-in and into a quiet, elegant lounge. A hostess showed Grace to a comfortable booth. She looked around as she waited for the hostess to bring her a coffee. The lounge was almost empty. In one corner, a couple chatted quietly, a little dog in a carrier at their feet. In another, an older man in a crisp suit worked on a laptop. Stephen returned from making a discreet lap of the lounge and sat opposite her.

Grace raised an eyebrow. "You're more than a driver."

"I have some additional training, yes."

"I see. Would that include security-related training?"

"It would indeed."

Grace nodded.

"Why are we flying privately?"

"It's much easier to manage a private aircraft from a security perspective."

Grace sat back, looking happier.

Stephen cocked his head and looked at her closely. "You didn't like the idea of taking a private plane just for convenience or enjoyment, did you?"

Grace shook her head. "No, it seems excessive. But I understand the security perspective. It makes me wonder why it's necessary, but I understand."

Stephen shrugged.

"Don't tell me – Mr Anderson will explain," Grace said, laughing.

Stephen smiled. "You beat me to it."

***

The small plane touched down gracefully on the runway. Grace yawned and stretched. Her plush leather seat had lent itself well to a nap. The lack of sleep the previous night had crept up on her, despite the coffee.

Stephen looked up from his book. Grace tilted her head to read the cover. It was a book about the battle of Waterloo.

"Military history buff?"

"I enjoy it. I'm no expert."

The sun shone brightly on the imposing rock that stood out behind the airport, covered with dark green trees and plants that contrasted with the pale stone.

A dark saloon was waiting for them in the car park. Stephen halted Grace as she approached and walked around the car, checking it carefully, before he unlocked it and put her luggage into the boot.

Grace raised an eyebrow. She really was accruing quite a number of questions for Mr William Anderson.

They drove through the streets. Grace had never been to Gibraltar before. It looked tired and dusty, like a theme park based on a British seaside town that had been left to bleach and dull in the intense sun.

The Mid-Harbour Marina was serene. The tower blocks of the town, backed by the rugged rock and trees, fell away behind them, and the sea lapped softly in the midday sun.

Sweat stung Grace's forehead as they stepped out of the coolness of the car. She'd worn her lightest summer suit, a trouser suit in navy, but even so, her blouse immediately clung to her skin.

Stephen pointed the way along the dock. Grace looked in the direction he was gesturing. Out at sea, behind several handsome sail yachts and fast-looking boats, was a floating city. The *Accidental Diamond* rose out of the water like a giant, glistening, pristine white iceberg.

"You weren't joking when you said she was big," Grace remarked.

Stephen snorted. "You'll probably get a little lost on her at first, but the captain will give you a guided tour."

Grace reviewed her knowledge of yachts. To her, they were synonymous with lavish, wasteful parties and thoughtless excess. If this was Mr Anderson's boat, how, she wondered, did he live his life? Eating caviar with oligarchs and sipping champagne out of supermodel's belly buttons, probably.

Grace frowned. She really had no idea what this assignment would entail or how this could be connected to her areas of experience. She'd worked hard to progress as a forensic psychologist before moving into a leadership role in the counter-corruption team within the prison service. Her work was fascinating, but far from glamorous.

"There's a RIB waiting to take us aboard," Stephen said.

"A rib?" Grace furrowed her brow. She'd grown up in the city. This nautical talk was well beyond her sphere of knowledge.

"RIB – Rigid Inflatable Boat."

"Ah…" said Grace, trying to sound like this explained things.

An athletic young woman waved to Stephen from a sleek craft bobbing at the quayside. He lowered their bags to her, climbed down and turned to guide Grace into the RIB. She took a seat on a bench under the shade of the canvas awning in the rear of the boat.

The blonde woman smiled warmly at Grace. "Good to meet you, Miss Adair. I'm Hayley."

Grace took her offered hand. Her hands were slender, but her grip was firm.

"You too, Hayley. And you can call me Grace, if that's appropriate. I don't know what yacht rules on names are."

Hayley winked. "We'll see once you've settled in, but let's stick with Miss Adair for now. Please hold on tight. We're heading off now."

Grace nodded. The triple engines whirred into life with a low hum. Water bubbled around them as they headed smoothly out of the marina towards the *Accidental Diamond*. The smell of gasoline mingled with the fresh salty tang of the sea, and Grace closed her eyes in pleasure at the novel scents – she spent so much time in the city, being at sea felt delightful.

As they moved out away from the other boats, Hayley accelerated hard. The RIB rose out of the water as they sliced swiftly through the sea. Grace clutched the bench, feeling the force of their speed pushing at her. She gasped and then laughed as the spray hit her face, and the sensation of their movement sent butterflies to her stomach. Hayley glanced back at her. Grace smiled and raised her hand, thumbs up.

Hayley raised her hand to radio a message, but her words were mainly snatched away by the wind. Stephen sat next to Grace, alert, eyes scanning the horizon, but with a smile playing on his lips.

Grace's dark hair had begun to unravel itself in the breeze. She smoothed it with her fingers, feeling tendrils already starting to curl against her neck in the salt spray, tying it back into a bun.

They drew nearer to the yacht. The water slapped loudly against the hull as they approached. Hayley signalled to two men, and Stephen threw the stern and bow lines into their waiting hands. Hayley manoeuvred the RIB forward, and the lines held it tightly against the stern of the *Accidental Diamond*. Grace took one of the men's hands and stepped off, her legs shaking a little as she walked up onto the deck. She thanked him and turned to look around her.

Stephen put a pair of navy canvas shoes down next to her. "Put these on, please, Miss Adair."

Grace looked at them quizzically.

"When on board, we wear deck shoes to protect the wood of the decks," he said, pointing to the black pair he had just put on.

"It had never occurred to me that was why deck shoes were called that. How did you know what size to get me?"

"Mr Anderson ordered them."

Grace shook her head and put them on. She felt the warm, soft nose against her arm before she saw the dog. She looked up quickly. And up. In her position, crouched on the deck, the silver-grey dog towered over her. There was a ball at its feet. She fussed the dog, smiling as it licked her hands and glanced at the tag on the collar.

"Good dog, Morrigan. Do you want your ball thrown?" Grace rolled the ball gently along the deck. Morrigan ran after it, tail wagging wildly. Paws clattered along the decking and a second dog, just like Morrigan, came to join the fun, sniffing at Grace's feet. She reached out and petted it. This one's collar tag read "Aurora." They were beautiful dogs, large, graceful and well-muscled.

"Who do the dogs belong to?" she asked Stephen.

"Mr Anderson. The girls come everywhere with him if he can possibly arrange it." He smiled at them indulgently, as they ran to him. Morrigan collapsed onto her back with a complete lack of dignity given her size and noble demeanour, waiting for her belly to be rubbed. Stephen gave the dogs a final pet, then waved and headed off below deck with his bags.

One of the staff took her shoes, along with her luggage, and guided her down to the staterooms. "This is your cabin. Please make yourself at home," she said, placing Grace's bags on the luggage rack. "The captain will collect you in an hour for a tour of the boat before he takes you to meet Mr Anderson for lunch."

"Thanks."

Grace looked around. Her cabin held an elegant king-size bed made up in soft, cool blue linen. The ensuite was lavishly furnished. She ran her fingers over the smooth woods, marble and fine fabrics around her. She couldn't recall ever staying in a hotel as well-appointed. She took a long shower and changed into a simple long black dress with cap sleeves, sweeping her hair back smoothly. Grace added a sweep of eyeliner, and a touch of blusher to her cheeks. Feeling cooler and fresher, she sat down on a handsome wingback armchair next to the porthole and looked out at the sea. They had begun to move away from Gibraltar, and the water sparkled in the sunshine. Seagulls wheeled above them, their white shapes thin lines in the bright blue of the sky. A gentle knock sounded at the door. Grace rose and opened it.

"Miss Adair, I'm Captain Tom Rogers." A red-haired man stepped forward, dressed in a crisp uniform with golden epaulettes on the shoulders. Grace shook his hand. "Let me show you around." The captain led her onto the main deck.

Grace surveyed her surroundings with interest as he explained the layout of the yacht to her. The woods of the flooring and fixtures glistened with care, and white sun loungers and chairs looked inviting and immaculate under canvas awnings. A blue-tiled pool gave a view out to sea. A bar was positioned next to a rather grand covered dining area, with a ceiling of twinkling crystals arranged in constellations against a deep blue backdrop to emulate the night sky.

They headed inside and Grace lost count of the rooms as they explored further. It reminded her of being shown around a stately home – and indeed, the inside of the yacht had a classic, understated beauty that gave her the sense that she could as easily be in a Georgian mansion as on a boat. The grand salon, a library, a great dining room, a lounge, suites of staterooms and cabins. They walked past a section that the captain did not mention.

"What is through there?" Grace asked.

"Those are the functional and crew areas," Tom said. He steered her towards the salon. "Mr Anderson will be down to meet you for your briefing and for lunch shortly." He indicated a seat on a comfortable sofa, next to a table where a selection of books, bottles of iced water and a platter of beautifully presented fruit awaited her.

Grace sat down and explored the books. There was a heavy academic volume of military history – Stephen's tastes were catered for, at least. An antique hardback copy of the poetry of Samuel Taylor Coleridge and a beautifully illustrated book of haiku caught her eye.

She leafed through the haiku. A lovely brush painting of tall grasses against a full moon accompanied a Basho poem, one of her favourites:

Summer grasses –
All that remains
Of warriors' dreams.

Fitting, with the military history book, she thought.

"You enjoy reading haiku?"

Grace turned. William leaned against the doorframe behind her, dressed in a light serge navy suit with a casual sea island cotton polo shirt underneath. She had not heard him come in, but years of working in prisons meant that she rarely startled at unexpected noises.

"Yes. I write them, too, occasionally, only for my own pleasure, not for publication."

He nodded. "Writing for your own pleasure is the greatest reason for writing. Everything else comes second."

"Do you write?" Grace asked. She could not imagine him engaging in such quiet, studious pursuits.

William smiled. "I have often wanted to, and thought of doing so, but have had little opportunity since leaving university."

"What did you study?"

"Philosophy, politics and economics."

"Ah, the classic PPE. I'm surprised you didn't go into politics."

"No, the military held a greater pull for me at that stage in life. How about you? Did you go straight into psychology?"

"Yes, undergrad degree, followed by a Master's in Forensic Psychology, then a postgraduate qualification to grant me my registration."

"I understand that Forensic Psychology is a competitive field."

"Yes, getting to the point of qualification is challenging and requires a lot of persistence. It is easier once you qualify. What was your regiment? Household Cavalry?"

"The Blues and Royals – what gave the equine connection away?"

"Partly the photos in the governor's office, his tie pin and partly the digging I did talking to Stephen on the way over."

William laughed.

"Speaking of digging, how did you know what size shoes to get me?"

"Ah, that is one of many secrets of the Moonlight Society."

Grace frowned. "The Moonlight Society? Who are the Moonlight Society – and what gives them the resources and powers to find out a little personal detail like that?"

William smiled. "I'm joking. I'm actually just rather good at guessing shoe and clothing sizes."

Grace raised an eyebrow. "And you have many occasions to guess the shoe and clothing sizes of women, of course."

William sat down on the sofa opposite her. "In my life as an international playboy, you mean?"

"Yes, well, the yacht rather suggests that sort of lifestyle."

William shook his head. "No, I actually just have a mother and sisters who I am close to and like to buy gifts for."

"Ah." Grace looked at the book she still held in her lap, running her thumb along the spine as she avoided his eye a little awkwardly.

"Now, you must be hungry. Let us go and have lunch, and I'll brief you while we eat. I thought you'd prefer to eat on deck rather than in the dining salon."

Grace followed William up onto the deck. He pulled out a chair for her at an elegant dining table under the cover of the jewelled galaxy canopy.

A soft breeze gentled the sun's intensity as they sat in the shade. Grace looked out across the sea. Gibraltar had faded into a pale line of mountains behind them, a stark contrast against the dark blue of the Alboran Sea.

"Where are we heading?" Grace asked as a hostess placed a napkin on her knees.

"Well, that is something we'll need to discuss, but for now, we're headed towards Málaga."

The hostess placed plates of a rich pâté, delicately sliced on thin slivers of bread, topped with tiny, sparkling pearls of quince jelly in front of them and poured glasses of ice-cold sherry.

"I am aware you must have rather a lot of questions, Grace. Where would you like to start?"

Grace sipped her drink thoughtfully. "Who are the Moonlight Society?"

William leaned back, turning the delicate stem of his crystal glass between his fingers as he considered his response.

"The Society has existed for three hundred years. It was initially made up primarily of aristocrats and the most powerful merchants from across Europe. We are a covert Society whose main purpose is to assist governments in investigating high-level crime and corruption. Our members are uniquely positioned to access parts of the social hierarchy that would traditionally be inaccessible to law enforcement and government agencies."

Grace frowned. "So, who governs your activity?"

"We do. There is a rigorous process of internal ethics audits and becoming a member of the Society requires a thorough investigation into your character, assets, activities and connections. We sit outside of government agencies, which allows us to conduct our work with a degree of freedom and discretion that would not normally be possible."

"I see."

"You don't look convinced. I understand your scepticism. Your specialism in counter-corruption work will rightly see our lack of external governance as a red flag. However, I hope that with time you will come to appreciate that our strong traditions of honour, integrity and justice inform all of our actions."

Grace inclined her head. "You referred to the positions of the other members of the Society – who are they?"

William smiled. "Ah, you will be meeting some of them soon enough – they will be joining us at Málaga. The Society is comprised of members whose specialist knowledge, power, prestige and social rank enable them to engage in our work with a unique freedom. We are called the Moonlight Society because our activity always takes place under the cover of a more eclipsing social role for the members. They are rock stars, entrepreneurs, inventors, CEOs of major corporations, aristocrats and artists. They are also brave, courageous and discreet."

Grace looked around the yacht. It was vast, glittering and lavish. It looked like something a Russian oligarch, or an oil tycoon would own. "Discreet?"

William raised a wry eyebrow.

"Where would a group of society's elite meet?"

Grace shrugged. "I guess a yacht makes sense."

"And a vast, lavish party aboard a superyacht makes an excellent cover for our activity."

"Why a yacht and not a fancy club in Marlborough or something?"

"Good question. The original Society headquarters were in a fine old club in London. Many of the antique books, furnishings and ornaments you'll see aboard were rescued from the old HQ building when it rather unfortunately burned down."

"Burned down? Accidentally?"

"More or less."

Grace decided to let that one go.

William waved a hand around expansively, his gesture taking in the spacious deck, with its pools, loungers, bar and dining areas and the sea beyond. "This serves both as an excellent cover for our seminars and provides a location for our HQ that is readily controllable from a security perspective."

Grace looked around with new eyes. There was essentially a built-in moat, the lines of sight were excellent, and communications could be controlled with ease.

She shut her eyes and put a finger to her lip in disbelief. For a long moment, she couldn't speak. "So, this is a floating fortress, a Trojan horse that looks like a pleasure barge but is actually a warship?"

"An excellent summary, although our capabilities are more defensive than offensive."

"And this Society of yours is an elite form of the Masons with a taste for crime-fighting?"

"Well, I'm less content with that analogy, but I suppose there are some justified parallels."

"So, when Elon Musk wants to play Batman, it's you he calls?"

"No, actually, Mr Musk was vetted but declined."

The hostess returned with a chilled bottle of water. Grace turned her attention to her plate, and they ate in silence. Once the waitress had taken their plates, Grace leaned forward and looked William squarely in the eye.

"What do you want from me? I'm not one of Society's elite. I'm not a billionaire or a world-ranking expert. Why am I here?"

William held her gaze, his grey eyes locked onto her green ones.

"I need an expert on counter-corruption. Ian is amongst the men I trust most in this world, and given the nature of his work, I knew that he would be able to send me someone with the highest level of integrity, with knowledge of wide-scale corruption and with the skill to support our work."

Grace blinked and dropped her eyes, cheeks beginning to flush. "I see."

The hostess brought them their main courses. Grace examined her plate curiously. There was a beautiful fillet of fish cushioned on a bed of roasted tomatoes, fennel and finely sliced potatoes. The menu sheet on the table announced it to be red mullet. The scents mingled, fresh, bright and clean. She raised her fork and began to eat. The dish was exquisite, the tastes well balanced, and the ingredients first class.

"Chef enjoys it when we are in the Mediterranean. He firmly believes that some of the finest produce and fish can be found here," William said.

Grace nodded.

William refilled their wine glasses. "Interpol have asked the Society to investigate a concerning development in the smuggling of illegally mined gold."

Grace waved her fork at him, which he took as a request for further details.

"Previously, the main flow of gold illegally mined in Africa came via Dubai, through the unsophisticated method of getting people to transport it in their hand luggage. Pressure on Dubai to address this increased sufficiently that the finance minister of the UAE proposed an international ban on transporting gold in hand luggage. Since this has been imposed, the illegal gold running through Dubai has slowed to a trickle, yet intelligence suggests that production in the illegal mines has increased."

"Tell me more about the illegal mines," Grace said.

"Across several regions, there are restrictions on mining. Mines must be regulated, should treat their staff well and should not pollute the environment. However, corruption has enabled illegal mining to flourish. Often the mines are run by local warlords or gangs. There are frequent injuries and fatalities, and sometimes the staff are forced to work for little or no money. The mining often causes significant damage to the landscape and waterways – but the profits are such that the mine owners are able to pay off local officials and government ministers, who turn a blind eye."

"So why do they need smugglers – and why Dubai?"

"The problem is that if the gold has not come through a recognised refinery, it is difficult to sell on. Most European countries will ask for a certificate of origin before agreeing to buy gold. However, in Dubai, there has been a somewhat more relaxed approach… which has meant that gold can be sold there, to be melted down and remade into jewellery and bullion. Once it is mixed with other golds, it becomes untraceable and can then bleed out into the global markets."

"It sounds like putting a snag in the Dubai route was a major problem for the mines – and for the people profiting in Dubai. There'll be some very annoyed people there who are losing a great deal of money," Grace said thoughtfully.

"Indeed. We don't know at this point how and where the gold is diverting to, but if it is not coming into Dubai, it must be going somewhere."

"If this was my investigation, I'd start asking questions in Dubai," Grace said.

William laughed. "Well, that is a sound idea. Welcome to the team. Several Society members with experience relevant to this investigation will join us in Málaga, and we will form a plan of action from there."

Chapter 4 – The Shoe Shiner

Brescia, Italy, 1970

The sun was low in the sky, throwing golden light over the handsome ornate brickwork of the railway station and on the people who hurried about the streets.

Francesco sat in the shade of one of the arched doorways of the main entrance, his folding stool and kit set out in front of him.

A young man in a well-worn suit stopped and greeted him. Francesco gestured for him to sit and set about cleaning and polishing the cheaply made shoes. He rubbed a little extra polish into a crack that was starting to open along the creased toe of the left shoe. He looked down. The young man had set down a bouquet of flowers next to the stool.

Francesco grinned. "Today's the day?" he asked.

The young man blushed and nodded.

"Good luck. I'm sure she'll say yes," Francesco said. He'd polished these shoes for an interview for a new job, for dates with the girl he was going to propose to. In a small way, he was part of this man's story.

He gave a final flourish of a rag to bring a shine to the shoes. Although old and worn, they looked respectable and clean.

The young man pressed some coins into Francesco's hand. "If she says yes, you'll be polishing my shoes for my wedding day," he said with a nervous smile.

Francesco waved him off, then, noticing he'd left the bouquet for his sweetheart next to Francesco's stool, chased after him.

The young man turned as Francesco called out to him and, seeing the flowers in his hands, slapped his hand on his forehead. "Thank you, thank you so much." He pulled another coin from his pocket and handed it to Francesco, squeezing his hand as he gave it to him.

Francesco put the coin into the pouch at his waist as the young man walked on. A heavy handful of coins trickled through his fingers between a few small notes. He smiled. He had taken the money Mr Rossi had given him for his mother and built a business. He had regular customers who visited him to have their shoes shined. They'd tell him about their day, about their business troubles and about their wives and children.

In the past two years, he must have shined thousands of shoes. He'd shined enough shoes to put food on the table when his father stopped coming back. Enough to save a little each week in an old tobacco tin behind a loose skirting board.

Mama had cried when he had brought home his first bag of groceries the same day that Mr Rossi had given him the money. He'd gone straight to buy a set of brushes and polish and to beg his elderly neighbour to lend him a stool and an orange box to put under his customers' feet as he shined their shoes. Francesco had stayed at the railway station until he finally had more money in his pocket than he'd started with. Packing up his kit, he had run to the store, despite his aching back, and filled a bag with fresh tomatoes, onions and as many good things as he could afford. And his mama had wept.

Francesco smiled at the memory. She had been so relieved that she could cook him a meal, that they could eat, but had scolded him for not going to school and for not telling her what he was doing.

He looked up. The sun was beginning to set as the last stragglers left the train on their way back from work. Francesco put his kit away and walked home.

His mother was at the sink when he opened the door of their small apartment, washing glasses to set the table with.

He sat down, happy to listen to her chatter. She still struggled with pain from her back but had been able to go back to work for a few hours each day, minding her old boss's children.

She put a bowl of soup and fresh bread in front of him. He breathed the fragrant steam with pleasure – chickpeas, onions and vegetables with little shreds of pork in a delicious broth flavoured with rosemary. The smell made his mouth water like nothing else did. This was the reason it was called *minestra dei morti* – the soup of the dead.

After he had cleared away the plates, his mother brought out a string bag of books she'd picked up from the library.

Francesco groaned and rolled his eyes, but his mother patted his seat at the table, and he reluctantly sat down.

Since he had stopped going to school, his mama had insisted that they spend each evening reading. They learned about different countries of the world, mathematics and science. His mama loved to read history, and Francesco didn't mind so much when they studied history. His mama's eyes shone when she talked about the glories of the pyramids, the ingenuity of the Roman Empire or the excesses of the French Revolution, but tonight it was a biology book.

Francesco yawned as he sat over the book, making notes on a scrap of paper in case his mother decided to test him on what he'd read, as she sometimes did.

His eyelids drooped. He took out the seashell he still carried in his pocket and turned it over and over in his fingers to help him to focus on the page before him.

His mother ran her fingers through his hair. "Come on, Francesco. One day you will be a great man, and great men need to know great things."

He smiled sleepily at her. "OK, Mama. But can I be a great man tomorrow? I'm so tired today."

She gave a small click of her tongue, her eyes soft despite the shake of her head. "Yes, Franco, go and wash and get ready for bed. But tomorrow will be a test day to make up for it."

Francesco lay down on his soft, well-worn sheets. His head swam with tiredness as he ran through his accounts in his head, counting on his fingers the money in his tobacco tin and the money he'd be able to save over the coming weeks. His face was washed, his clothes neatly folded, and his kit lay by the front door, ready for him to head out early the next morning.

He ran his fingernail along the contours of the seashell.

Tomorrow, he would be a great man.

Chapter 5 – The Team

The *Accidental Diamond* was berthed in San Andres Marina, looking out along a strip of bustling restaurants and bars. Grace stood on deck, gazing out towards the pretty boardwalks. The other Society members were due to join them and she was curious about their arrival.

A bustle of movement caught her eye. A group of people got out of two or three large black cars and were immediately surrounded by a flock of people. Three large men in dark T-shirts and sunglasses pushed the crowd back, and the car's occupants began to walk towards the yacht, followed by the trailing onlookers.

An impossibly beautiful tall black woman, a shorter bearded man wearing sunglasses and a man and a woman who seemed of less interest to the crowd made up the group. Grace looked at them again. She recognised the woman – it was Amira Jones, the supermodel! The man also looked familiar. Grace rolled her eyes. Gerrard Browning-Maynard, notorious playboy, entrepreneur and billionaire owner of a prominent technology company. The remaining two, she didn't recognise: a very stylish woman with dark bobbed hair and a slim sandy-haired man.

William joined her at the railing. "Ah, they are here."

"Yes. Indeed, they are," Grace replied.

William gave her a sidelong glance. "Amira and Gerrard, I guess you will recognise. The other two are Sarah, one of the most prominent jewellers in Europe, and Richard, an inventor and adventurer who serves as our general armourer and trouble-shooter."

"Armourer?"

"Well, sometimes our investigations can lead us into choppy waters. It is sensible for us to have the capability to defend ourselves."

"I see. I understand the presence of Sarah and Richard in the investigation team. I do not, however, understand the purpose of a model and frat-boy billionaire."

William smiled. "Amira is a talented scientist with a particular interest in physics, fluent in four languages and very well-connected in high society across Europe and the Middle East. Gerrard's technology company provides us with advanced intelligence and communications systems, and his knowledge of cybersecurity is almost unparalleled."

"Ah." Grace studied them as they approached the walkway to the yacht. "I may have judged them a little harshly."

William laughed. "You're meant to. Everyone is. That's the point of the Society. We are called the Moonlight Society because we all have a daytime occupation that draws attention elsewhere. Our motto is 'gloire sous le soleil, victoire sous la lune' – glory under the sun, victory under the moon. What we do in the Society, we do quietly. Our greatest victories are known only to ourselves, as are our losses, of course. The glitzy, lavish lifestyle is a mirage. It prevents people from looking and thinking any further than the champagne and diamonds."

Grace looked at him thoughtfully. "And, of course, this just looks like a party of models, billionaires and socialites."

"Exactly!" William clapped his hands. "It also happens to be Gerrard's birthday, so we'll leak some stories to the press about the excesses at our party, the thousand-dollar bottles of cognac we toasted him with, the masses of caviar, etc., etc."

Grace laughed. "I think I will be rather an obvious odd one out if the paparazzi manage to get any photos up here."

"Oh no, I've already thought about that. You are my mysterious brunette companion, believed to be the daughter of an oil tycoon."

"My father is an energy plant engineer."

"Well, that is close enough, is it not?"

"And I'm not your companion."

William leaned back on the railings and looked down at her. "Are you not? Well, I won't tell anyone if you won't." He winked and moved to her side, offering his arm. "Let us go and greet our guests."

Grace took his arm. She pinched the tender flesh on the inside of his bicep and felt him flinch.

He stifled a laugh. "I deserved that."

***

Grace watched as the team filed into the *Accidental Diamond*'s grand salon for a Moonlight Society business meeting. She sat on William's left, with Stephen on her right.

"Good morning, help yourself to coffee." William gestured to the table.

Grace held her cup tightly between her hands.

She looked around the table. Gerrard, Amira, Sarah, Richard – they all looked effortlessly elegant and polished. Nervousness wormed through her body, making her legs shake and sweat sting her underarms.

Get a grip, Grace. She'd assessed violent offenders for court – men who had killed, sometimes repeatedly. She'd sat quietly typing a report in her office as projectiles were hurled off the roof while the prison was in lockdown due to a full-scale riot. She'd brought down corrupt officers and large-scale smuggling operations in prisons across the country. A jeweller, a model, an adventurer and a billionaire entrepreneur should not be giving her a moment of anxiety.

"As discussed, Grace Adair will join us for this project. We are lucky to have been granted a secondment from her role as Counter-Corruption Lead in the prison service."

They all smiled, offering hands to shake as they introduced themselves.

Stephen nudged her gently with his elbow. She looked at him quizzically.

"You look like you're trying to strangle the life out of your mug," he whispered.

Grace smiled, loosening her grip on her coffee.

"Who would like to start?" William asked.

Richard cleared his throat and pulled a slide up on the screen. "This is our current arms inventory. As you can see, I've been increasing our store of non-lethals, carefully calibrated to meet the laws of countries we are most likely to be required to visit."

Grace frowned as she read.

Richard caught her eye. "The Moonlight Society try their best to stay out of trouble, but when it arises, it is my job to ensure that we are all well-equipped. Do you disapprove of weapons, Miss Adair?" His voice was crisp, to the point of sharpness.

She shook her head. "No, I understand the necessity. I'm just not used to civilians having access to them."

"Civilians?" Richard quirked his mouth in amusement. "Speak for yourself."

"I'm sorry–" Grace started to say.

Richard waved his hand airily. "No need to apologise. The position of the Society and its members is unique."

"If you can all let me know your measurements, I am in the process of 3-D printing custom ultra-thin body armour. It won't be ready for some time, but I anticipate it will add an almost weightless and invisible alternative to traditional Kevlar vests."

Grace stared at him. "Is that technology available to law enforcement and military forces?"

"No, it is my own invention. I collaborate with researchers worldwide in various government bodies, but at this stage, the armour would be too expensive to produce for wider use."

He pinned her with his gaze. "Any further questions, Miss Adair?"

She shook her head. She was making a mess of this. Best-case scenario, they'd think she was hopelessly out of her depth. Worst-case scenario, they'd think she was hopelessly out of her depth and incredibly rude.

Grace listened quietly as the rest of the team gave their updates on Society business. Amira had engaged in intelligence gathering through her contacts in the fashion world and hoped to be able to help Interpol build a case to break a human trafficking ring. Sarah and Gerrard had been assembling a dossier of evidence against a prominent jeweller in New York suspected of participating in money laundering. They all gave their reports with efficiency and attention to detail.

She thought back to William's pep talk about her role in the team. She doubted she could bring much to this table.

William was briefing them on his conversation with Jurgen. "Let's reconvene when we have had time to think further about the Dubai gold-smuggling issue and can formulate a plan of action."

They dispersed, William and Stephen remaining at the table, talking.

Grace went out onto the upper deck, desperate for some air. She hadn't felt like this since she was a trainee.

The railings felt cold against her skin. She rested her arms and forehead against the coolness of the metal.

"That was a lot to take in, huh?" Sarah joined her at the railings.

Amira walked over too. Grace hastily straightened up.

"I felt like an imposter when I went to my first Society meeting," Amira said, with a smile that Grace couldn't help returning, despite the grey cloud over her mood.

"Urgh, I was so out of my depth," she said, smoothing her hands over her hair. She could feel curls forming under her fingers from the spray, refusing to be tucked back into her neat braid.

"No, you weren't. It was just your first meeting," Sarah said, putting her arm through Grace's.

"Listen, the rising tide lifts all boats – we're all here to help each other out. Don't ever worry about being out of your depth."

"Everyone is happy to have you on the team," Amira added. "And we can't wait to hear about your job – forensic psychologist? That must be fascinating."

Grace laughed. "It's interesting, but there's a lot more paperwork than there is on TV."

Amira chuckled. "I guess it would be boring watching if half of the episode was someone filling out incident logs and writing reports."

"I think your jobs are probably more interesting." Grace shrugged.

"Well, our Moonlight Society work is fascinating, that's why we do it, to add some purpose and interest to constantly attending parties and events, but everything about your work must be so intriguing. You must see the very worst of what people are capable of," Amira said earnestly.

"And sometimes the very best," Grace replied. "It's an unusual way to make a living."

"Let's go and grab a drink, and you can tell us all about it – minus the paperwork," Sarah said, steering them towards the bar.

Chapter 6 – One Man's Trash

Brescia, Italy, 1978

It was cool in the shade of the train station. There were few people around this early, and the bells of the church echoed through the quiet streets.

Francesco smiled. He'd always enjoyed this part of the day, with just the familiar faces of shop

owners and traders around, setting up for the day's trade. His eyes wandered fondly over the

contents of the little shoeshine kit. The brushes were worn but still dependable. The old stool he had borrowed from a neighbour had been replaced with one he had purchased second-hand at the market.

A skinny child with grazed knees sat back and smiled proudly as he gestured to Francesco's boots. Francesco nodded in approval.

"Well done, Pasquale. I couldn't have done any better myself."

The boy clapped in delight.

"Are you sure I can keep all of this?" He gazed down on the polishes and brushes as if he had just been gifted a puppy.

"Yes, I have told my customers you'll be taking over the stall." Francesco put his hand on Pasquale's shoulder. "Work hard, now, but don't forget about your books."

He flipped a coin in the air. Pasquale caught it and tucked it into the bag at his waist.

"Thank you, I won't let you down," the boy said, turning back to arrange his kit.

Francesco stood and shook his trouser legs neatly into place before he walked on through the peaceful streets.

A garbage truck was parked near the church. A middle-aged man sat in the driver's seat, a newspaper spread over the wheel. A young man, stocky with unruly dark curls, leaned against the church railings, smoking.

He waved his hand, half in greeting and half to flick ash from the tip of his cigarette. "I'm Carlo."

"Franco."

They shook hands.

"Matteo is up front. We have our round to do, but first, let's get coffee. Drinks are on you today, new boy." Carlo grinned.

They jumped into the truck, Carlo and Francesco sharing the bench seat next to the driver. Francesco reached over to shake Matteo's hand. The older man took his hand and acknowledged him with a gruff nod before starting the engine.

Carlo wound down the window and propped his elbow against it.

"Our job is easy – collect garbage, drop it off. If we get through our round quickly, we still get paid the same and then we can knock off for the day–" Carlo broke off, his attention caught by a pretty blonde woman opening the shutters of a shop.

"Good morning, beautiful!" he called.

She called out a brief, polite reply, then continued to unlock the store, ignoring Carlo, despite him fixing his eyes on her and craning out the window as they passed. He shrugged.

"And then we can enjoy doing whatever it is we like to do best, which sure as hell isn't hauling garbage." He lit another cigarette. The breeze blew the smoke back into the cab of the truck.

Francesco smothered a cough.

Matteo pulled in on a side street, and they jumped out. Carlo ordered three espressos at the counter of a small open-sided coffee bar.

Carlo and Francesco chatted casually about football, Matteo occasionally joining in as they drank their coffee.

Francesco put his hand into his pocket to pay as they finished up.

Carlo put his hand on his sleeve. "No need. This one is on Matteo. You didn't really think I'd make you pay for coffee on your first day, did you?" He winked, chuckling, as he turned away.

Matteo rolled his eyes and pulled out a handful of coins.

Carlo put his arm around Francesco's shoulders as they walked out. "Don't worry, I'll show you the ropes. Matteo is too old, lazy and too much of a stick in the mud for any enjoyment, but we'll make our days as fun as we can, OK?"

"OK."

The day started warming up as the sun reached the narrow streets.

As they worked their way through their rounds, Carlo sang snatches of song in a fine tenor voice. Francesco joined in, adding harmonies. They earned applause and compliments from passers-by, with Carlo missing no opportunity to flirt with women who stopped to listen to them sing.

The morning passed quickly. Francesco found that he was enjoying himself. He quickly added up the money he'd earn this week with the shifts he'd agreed. When he got his first pay packet, he'd have enough to buy a little gift for his mama, some of the chocolates she liked, perhaps, and he'd still have money to put by.

"How do we get paid?" he asked Carlo.

"The boss brings our envelopes down on a Friday, but honestly, there's never enough cash in them for my taste."

"It doesn't seem a bad wage."

"Maybe, if you don't want more out of life than to pay your bills and go to the cinema once a week. We get paid peanuts, but there's good money to be made out here if you have a little imagination," Carlo said. "It's easy to top up your wages with very little effort."

"Do we get tips or something?" Francesco asked, frowning.

"Sort of. You'll see. A lot of people need to get rid of rubbish and are willing to pay someone to take it away. They don't ask questions, neither do we."

"I don't understand how that would make money."

Carlo smiled. "The government has strict rules about what can be disposed of and where it can go. Sometimes businesses need to get rid of waste that the government wants to charge them a lot of money for. We take it off their hands and find a home for it."

"Like reusing old furniture?"

Carlo glanced at Francesco, eyes narrowed, unsure if he was serious.

"Yeah, sure. Like reusing old furniture. Anyway, I could use an extra pair of hands to run some errands after our shift. Matteo isn't interested. You want in?"

Francesco looked at Carlo. He was a good-looking young man. Nice clothes, considering they were collecting garbage. He had easy manners and sharp eyes. Francesco liked him, but he'd learned a lot about people, shining shoes. After a while, you got good at spotting who could be trusted and who couldn't. Carlo was fun, but he wasn't sure how far he'd trust him.

He stopped and turned to face him. "Carlo, I like you and what you do is your own business, but I don't want to be involved in anything that could lead to trouble."

Carlo spread his hands wide. "Listen, there's no chance of trouble. This is just a bit of extra work that lines our pockets. Everyone knows, our bosses know, the government knows. It's just easier this way."

"Thank you for asking me. I appreciate it. I will always work hard, and we'll have fun on our rounds, but I'm not interested in being involved in any… additional business opportunities."

Carlo shrugged, a disarming grin on his face. "I bet you'll change your mind when you see how much money I'm bringing in on top of my wages."

"What sort of money are we talking? Enough money to buy a house?"

"Enough money to buy a house?" Carlo raised his eyebrows in mock disdain. "Listen, soon I'll have enough money to buy a house, then I'll have enough money to buy my mama a house. Then I'll have enough money to marry Sophia Loren."

"You're too late. She's already married."

"Then I'll marry her sister. You get the idea."

Francesco nodded. "I do. I understand. I'm saving money too. I want to go into business one day when I have enough money, but I want to do it the right way."

"You want to do it the slow way, you mean." Carlo rolled his eyes.

"Maybe, but I hope we both get to where we want to go, even if we take different roads."

"Sophia Loren's sister will be married by the time you've earned any good money, travelling by your road. Don't say I didn't warn you."

"I hate to be the one to tell you, but her sister is married to Mussolini's son."

"You're ruining my dreams, Franco, ruining them."

They laughed, clapping each other on the back, until Matteo beeped the truck's horn, shouting at them to stop playing around and get in.

Chapter 7 – Málaga to Dubai

Grace rolled her shoulders. They were tight. The flight to Dubai had been long, and despite the comforts of the jet, she just wanted to lie down and sleep.

She reflected on the past 24 hours. The briefing with the Moonlight Society members had been fascinating. They had rapidly reviewed the intelligence available to them, discussed how the resources of the Society could be deployed and formulated a plan. Gerrard had put his team to work in monitoring the internet and communications networks for possible patterns of activity around areas known to be prominent illegal mining regions. Amira had briefed them on the gold refining process and the equipment and infrastructure that would be necessary to smelt the gold and send it out into the world. Her information would help to identify potential industry players with the capacity to engage in dealing with the gold outside of the highly controlled registered refineries. They had agreed that Gerrard and Amira would remain in Europe, gathering information, whilst Grace, William, Richard and Sarah would go on to Dubai to assess the situation there.

Grace's previous experience in corruption investi–gations had given her a clear sense that where someone had lost out to a new face in town, there would be people whose empty pockets and hurt pride made them willing to talk – and whilst everyone said that they didn't snitch, most people would when the conditions were right.

William had secured a hotel suite for them. The whole top floor was set aside for use by Society staff. Stephen showed her to her room, which looked out onto the sea, the lights of Dubai glittering on the water in the fading light. The room was furnished in sleek black neutral tones, leather panelled closets lining one wall and the other taken up by an astonishingly large bed. Grace completed her usual hotel room ritual of opening and shutting all of the drawers and cupboards to see what interesting items they contained. The bedside drawers had little of note. A sewing kit, a hardback hotel guidebook and a neatly stacked pile of monogrammed paper and pens. A thick, fluffy robe hung on the back of the bedroom door and slippers were placed next to the bed. Grace turned to the closet. She opened the door. It was filled with dresses, shoes and suits. She shut the door and opened the second closet. There were handbags and jewellery cases.

"Stephen," she called.

"Something wrong?"

"No, but I think maybe you've put me in the wrong room. There are clothes in the wardrobe."

Stephen smothered a smile. "No, that's definitely your room."

Grace frowned. "Am I sharing it with another member of staff?"

"No, it's just for you."

"Then why are there clothes in there that aren't mine?"

"Those are… your uniform."

"My what?"

"Your uniform. There will be several social engagements and events that you are required to attend, so Mr Anderson had one of the Society members in Dubai ensure you had adequate clothing for them."

Grace swore under her breath. "Has he seen *The Thomas Crown Affair*, by any chance?"

Stephen shrugged. "It's just part of the job."

"Well, I would at least have liked to have chosen my own clothes."

"The first engagement is in two hours, so Mr Anderson thought this would be more convenient."

Grace sighed. "OK, where are we going, and what is the dress code?"

"Black-tie dinner at an underwater restaurant. Mr Anderson will brief you in the car on the way."

Grace pressed her lips together. "An underwater restaurant? Why not go all out and go for a casino!"

"There are no legal casinos in Dubai, but Oceana is one of the finest restaurants in the region," Stephen replied.

"Unbelievable. A couple of days ago, I was sitting in a prison boardroom. Now I'm going to have to wear stilettos at an under-the-sea black-tie dinner. You know we aren't even allowed to wear high heels in the prison in case we have to run, Stephen? This is a pretty rapid change of gear."

She stalked off to her room, pretending not to hear Stephen's snort of laughter behind her.

***

The elaborately set tables sat in pools of light from sparkling chandeliers. Floor-to-ceiling windows into the sea filled the room with an intense, undulating blue light. Brightly coloured fish flashed amongst silken ribbons of seaweed. Occasional darker, larger shadows suggested predators lurked in the depths.

Grace's eyes were bright with interest as she glanced around the dining room. She had chosen a black dress with an elegant neckline that left her shoulders bare, with the two straps crossing over her collarbones. Even in a pair of very high, stylish peep-toe shoes, Grace's head only came to the top of William's shoulder.

A pair of diamond teardrop-shaped earrings shone like stars against the dark of her hair. William nodded in approval. Grace smiled at him. She had thanked him a little curtly for stocking her wardrobes with clothes, shoes and jewellery, but he was right. She needed to be dressed appropriately for their work, and frankly, she would have been at a loss picking out what to wear. So, accepting this, she had chosen her outfit with careful attention to detail.

A waiter showed them to their table. Sarah and Richard were already at the table and stood to welcome them. A third man, tall, serious and lavishly dressed, rose from the table to shake William's hand and incline his head to Grace.

This, Grace thought, must be Khalid Ali, Sarah's contact in Dubai.

They took their seats.

Sarah reached forward to touch Grace's earrings. "Do you like them? They are a vintage Harry Winston pair that I knew one of my contacts here owned after he picked them up at auction last year. I asked for them specifically for you. I thought they'd suit you."

Grace smiled. "They are stunning, but I'm terrified wearing them. I looked up Harry Winston when I saw the name on the box. These things must have literally cost a fortune."

Sarah squeezed her hand. "Harry Winston wasn't called the King of Diamonds for nothing. But don't worry, they are insured – and this is all part of making sure you look the part over here."

Grace nodded. "I'll still be glad to give them back."

They turned their attention back to the table.

Waiters had delivered a starter of transparent slivers of octopus carpaccio, topped with a scattering of miniature flowers and herbs, to create a little jewel box on the plate. It was, Grace thought, like a snack for a particularly dainty mermaid.

Khalid chatted amiably, but his eyes were alert., constantly scanning, always conscious of who was around their table.

He leaned forward. "Those are some very fine earrings, Miss Adair. Mr Anderson chose well for you."

"Sarah chose well for me. On behalf of Mr Anderson, of course."

"Then Mr Anderson chooses his advisors well."

"You are a jeweller too, I believe," Grace said.

Khalid inclined his head. "Yes, I am. Like Sarah, I have always had a thirst for things that shine and sparkle."

Grace moved her lips towards his ear. "I heard that certain new rules have created some difficulties for those in Dubai seeking to make their living from that which sparkles and shines."

Khalid drew back and appraised her. William was talking softly to Richard, whilst observing her from his peripheral vision.

Khalid smiled. "Yes, some noses are out of joint. I myself have always traded primarily in stones, and those are so closely regulated that it is not worth my while to dabble in smuggling."

"But those whose noses are out of joint must be wondering where the gold that used to flow through Dubai is going now."

"That is the question which many mouths debate."

"Do you think any of those mouths might be willing to talk?"

Khalid tapped his fingers thoughtfully on his chin. "It depends on why you want to talk to them."

William turned to face Khalid.

Khalid drew back from Grace a little.

"We are curious about where the gold leaving Africa is going if it isn't coming to Dubai. And whilst our aims are not those of the people in Dubai, we share a common desire to ensure that this other route is dammed up," William said, his voice smooth and conversational.

Khalid nodded. "Some friends and I will be attending the races tomorrow. I am sure there is space in the box for you and Miss Adair."

William smiled and offered his hand. "My thanks, Mr Ali. We shall be delighted to join you."

***

Grace dressed in a cream linen shirt dress from her new wardrobe. It was cut exquisitely and looked refined and cool with a simple leather belt that complemented her high court shoes and clutch. Grace rubbed the balls of her feet before she put them on. It had been years since she'd worn high-heeled shoes on a regular basis, and her calf muscles and feet complained at the abrupt change in footwear.

Sarah sat at her dressing table, rifling through the jewel cases she'd brought with her. She took out a diamond tennis bracelet and a pair of diamond studs and put them on for Grace. "There. Perfect for a day at the races."

"How do people make this much effort to get dressed every day? I don't own a single piece of gold or diamond jewellery, except for an antique watch my neighbour gave me when his wife died. There's rarely even the occasion to wear the watch. Prisons aren't the place to wear glamorous jewels."

"Well, a lot of the people who make this much effort to get dressed don't have too much else to do. And that is the look we want to achieve for you."

Grace grinned. "Daughter of an oil tycoon, right?"

"Right."

There was a knock at the door.

"Come in," Grace called.

Richard came in, carrying a leather case.

"Oh please, no, not more jewellery or handbags," Grace said.

"No." Richard smiled. "Not really my department." He laid the case on the bed and opened it. Inside lay a slim, ornate crystal bottle.

"Perfume?" Grace said, reaching out to pick it up.

Richard halted her hand. "To all intents and purposes, yes. It would pass any inspection as a perfume; however, the delivery system, when you press the spray head continuously, is rather high-powered, and the liquid, whilst pleasantly scented, is exceptionally irritating to eyes and would incapacitate an attacker immediately."

"Is pepper spray legal here?"

"This isn't pepper spray. It's merely a perfume with added features. Keep it with you," Richard said.

"Can I wear it as perfume?"

"I wouldn't recommend it. I did my best with the scent blending, but it's a little heavy on the musk. It should be convincing enough if you were required to spray it to demonstrate its innocuousness, though."

"OK, where do I put it?" Grace said. "I can't put it on my belt, and I don't have space in this little bag."

"I had anticipated that problem." Richard held out a sheath tucked into a pocket in a black lace tube.

"Is this a pair of knickers with a hidden pocket?" Grace said, frowning at it.

"Nope, thigh holster," Richard said, demonstrating how the lace fitted by holding it up to one of his own thighs, which it would clearly fail to encircle.

"The bottle is of a very robust glass. It will not show on any metal scanner, and the holster will not be visible under your dress. It is just in case there are any… difficulties during your trip."

"Are we anticipating difficulties? Because I learned the basics to protect myself in the prison self-defence programme, but they do not teach us offensive attacks, and civilians aren't trained to use PAVA spray."

"SPEAR?" Richard asked.

"Yes," Grace said.

"I prefer Krav Maga. But yes, I understand. This is purely a weapon of last resort. Mr Anderson and Stephen will be with you."

"Will they be armed?" Grace asked.

"Only with their own skills."

Grace let out a soft whistle.

"I am not going to ask any further questions." She sat down and secured the holster to her thigh. It fit smoothly under her skirt like a garter. She was beginning to regret not making more regular visits to the prison dojo as she contemplated the prospect of perhaps having to use the noxious spray.

"You could have got me one in cream lace to match my outfit, Richard."

"I'll make it in a few different colours," he said promptly.

"You made the holster, too?" Grace said.

"Yes, well, I like to keep busy." He picked up the case and snapped it shut.

Stephen appeared at the door. "Ready?"

"Ready."

William was waiting in the car by the steps to the hotel. He was dressed in a blue linen suit with a white shirt. Grace's heart quickened a little. He was handsome. Alarmingly so. His brown hair, enhanced by a fleck of grey, fell onto the forehead of a face that somehow managed to be beautiful and utterly masculine. The lines of his profile were hard and a little uncompromising, but his eyes were kind. Grace dismissed any thoughts about his attractiveness. This was business.

In the car, William handed her a slim file. "Gerrard has generated a profile for each of the men we are meeting today. Mr Ali sends his excuses, so it will just be his associates. There are none who I think we should be concerned about from a security perspective. Still, all have substantial business interests which deviate from what would be considered strictly legal in the gold industry."

Grace perused the pages.

"I doubt they have direct knowledge of where else the gold is going," William continued, smoothing his jacket.

Grace leaned forward to brush a piece of lint off his shoulder and blushed when he held her eye for a long moment as she reached out to him.

"But if there is gossip flying around, I think they'll be willing to tell us."

Grace nodded. "Yes, the losses of income must amount to millions. I can't imagine that any of the Dubai people who were complicit in profiting from smuggled gold will be pleased to find that the money is finding its way into other pockets."

The car pulled into the racecourse. It was filled with supercars, high-performance vehicles, stately chauffeur-driven classics and discreetly armoured SUVs.

Their box was large, well-shaded and with an excellent view down the track from the balcony. A dining table was laid with canapés, and a waiter offered them the choice of champagne or sparking apple juice as they entered. Grace took a glass of champagne and joined the knot of men on the balcony. A small, stocky man, who she recognised from his profile as Bashir Aziz, greeted her warmly and waved her to his side.

William joined the group.

"We'll have a good show today, some fine horses down there." Bashir grinned, clapping his hand on William's shoulder.

Horses walked around the paddock below them, displaying their form, their jockeys waiting to mount. Owners, punters and trainers milled around, waiting for the race to start.

Grace tried to keep an ear on William's conversation whilst attending to the enthusiastic and cheerful Bashir, who, on learning that she had never been to a horse race before, pointed out various sights, horses, jockeys and trainers.

William was talking about his horses. Grace's interest sharpened. She found it very difficult to get a clear sense of this powerful, complex man and his many interests.

"Of course, Stephen and several other of my former cavalry colleagues have helped to build the reputation of my stud significantly. Sales of our horses are doing well, both in Ireland and abroad."

The two men William was speaking with nodded, and they gathered together, sharing photos and videos of horses on their phones. William extracted his own phone from his inside pocket. Grace saw a picture of William astride a fine roan horse. She smothered a smile. He wore tight riding breeches and boots, not unlike his cavalry uniform. It reminded her strongly of Regency menswear, and she couldn't deny that her thoughts were suddenly flooded with an image of William as the hero of a Jane Austen novel. Captain Wentworth, most likely, although Colonel Brandon was also a contender.

Glancing up, he saw her looking at the photo and politely handed her the phone.

"What's the horse's name?" she asked, trying to appear nonchalant.

"Casanova."

She raised her eyes to him and lifted her brow incredulously.

He shrugged and leaned forward to whisper into her ear. "I have a reputation to maintain, remember!" He winked and turned away, returning to the conversation.

William was discussing the cost of freight to transport horses, the latest bloodlines and the prices of recently traded foals. "Of course, horses are a good option for investment," he said. "Especially as I hear that the gold trade has become less profitable here."

The tall man standing next to him, Taimoor Shah, a property investor, Grace remembered from his file, shrugged and gave a wry smile. "You are not wrong. Since the minister introduced the change to the law, the flow of well-priced gold has slowed down to an inconvenient extent, so yes, horses seem a better option right now."

William inclined his head in agreement. He turned to face the track, looking out across the crowds, and said casually, "I wonder where all that gold is going now."

Bashir turned to face him. "Oh, it must be going somewhere – and so must the money earned from it. If it is not coming through Dubai, my best bet is that someone in Europe has found a good loophole."

Taimoor made a noise of agreement.

"What makes you say that?" William said.

"One of my men attended an auction of diamonds and gemstones in Paris," Taimoor said. "He said that each of the best diamonds of two carats or more were snapped up by a mysterious buyer who had sent someone to bid on their behalf." He pulled out his phone and showed a blurry photo of a blonde-haired man in a dark suit. "We were intending to buy several of those stones and didn't get a look-in. My buyer sent me this photo. Neither of us recognises him."

"And the same thing happened when I attended an auction in Cologne!" Bashir chipped in.

"Each of the nicest stones went to an unknown buyer, but not the man in that photo; this was a dark-haired man. I have a contact there who works at the auction house. We went for drinks, and she told me that the diamonds were being sent to Switzerland, but that the buyer had mentioned that he was returning to Majorca."

Taimoor nodded. "And my buyer said that on asking around, the French diamonds were bound for Switzerland too, although the buyer seemed to be Italian. We're hearing of some big-ticket diamonds across Europe going to buyers no one is familiar with… and Switzerland seems to be the one common factor."

William looked at the men thoughtfully. "So, who do we think this new buying power is? A Mafia family from Majorca or one of the other big crime syndicates in Europe?"

He exchanged glances with Grace. Majorca could be a possible lead. It was known as a centre where European crime syndicates converged.

Taimoor shook his head. "No, I don't think so, or at least not directly. My guy asked around about the buyer at the auction house, and he didn't seem to be known to anyone – and neither was the buyer at the Cologne auction. There don't seem to be obvious links to known Mafia figures."

Bashir shrugged. "Whoever it is, they are making big money that they are keen to spend. I'd be surprised if they aren't linked to this new gold route. And it's galling. Not only are they making that money I used to make, but they are also using it to buy up stones I'd like to buy myself."

William took a sip from his drink. "I can see how that would be irritating."

Chapter 8 – A Debt Repaid

Brescia, Italy, 1985

Francesco looked up at the old factory. It stood tall and dusty, the neat paintwork faded by the sun of many summers. His father was long since dead, but the factory had carried on. The rhythm of men arriving for their morning shifts, chatting at the gates as they lined up, walking home in the cool of the evening, and the pounding of the machines had persisted through fair weather and foul in the city, and every day, Francesco had looked up at it and remembered Mr Rossi.

He pushed open the door and looked around. It had been smartened up – the old factory had not had a reception, but the new administration block provided sales and executive space and required a front desk.

"Could you tell me, is Mr Rossi at work today?" he asked the young receptionist.

She nodded and rose to point the way to the foreman's office.

Francesco strolled down the factory floor. A metallic tang filled the air and bright sparks lit the workstations on the far side. He knocked on the open office door.

A late-middle-aged man looked up at him from a ledger. He was older and thinner than the last time Francesco had seen him, but the tall frame and kind eyes were recognisable.

"Mr Rossi?"

"Yes, come in. How can I help you?" Mr Rossi moved a pile of paperwork from a chair, looked at Francesco's expensive suit and hastily dusted it down with a handkerchief before offering him a seat.

"I owe you breakfast."

Mr Rossi tilted his head to the side with a laugh. "Breakfast?"

"Yes. Many years ago, you gave me bread and some money, and I promised I'd pay you back one day. You said I could get you breakfast when I was older."

Mr Rossi beamed. "Antonio Castelli's boy. Francesco, was it?"

Francesco smiled. "Yes, Francesco. Let's take a walk to a café, shall we? Which do you like best?"

"Oh–" Mr Rossi reached out and patted his shoulder "–you don't have to do that. It's just a pleasure to see you grown up and looking so smart! Besides, I can't leave work; the factory has a new owner who is due to visit today. I was just checking over the ledgers before he arrives."

"Have they announced who the new owner is?" Francesco asked.

"No." Mr Rossi shook his head. "But I want to make a good impression."

"You did that with an act of kindness many years ago," Francesco said quietly.

Mr Rossi narrowed his eyes and frowned. He looked Francesco over from head to toe, taking in the elegant suit, handmade shoes, fine gold watch and immaculately cut hair.

He smiled and shook his head, his face lighting up with surprise and delight.

"Well, I guess we'll be getting breakfast then, Mr Castelli. I think we have some catching up to do."

"Francesco, please, Mr Rossi."

***

Mr Rossi drank the last of his coffee and sat back, content.

"How is your daughter?" Francesco asked. "She must be near my age, from what I can recall."

Mr Rossi's face clouded over. "My poor Laura. She had a terrible fall on the stairs in our apartment block two years ago. She broke her neck and couldn't move for months. She has regained some movement and strength, but she needs more physiotherapy and support to rebuild her muscles, and there's not enough available."

Francesco put his hands to his mouth, filled with sadness for the kind man before him.

"I am so sorry, Mr Rossi. Your wife must be heartbroken, too."

Mr Rossi sighed. "We lost her six months ago to cancer. It has been even harder since then, because Laura has no one to help her with her exercises during the day. I do my best at night, but it is not enough."

Francesco pressed his hands together in front of him, deep in thought. He remembered Laura. She was a merry, sweet-faced girl with thick, dark curls. He had seen her in church sometimes when they were children. He reached into his pocket.

Mr Rossi put his hand on his sleeve.

"No, no, let me get you breakfast to celebrate your success."

Francesco shook his head. "No, please, this is a pleasure that I have looked forward to every day since I was eight years old. I took the money you gave me and used it to buy a shoeshine kit, and that was my first business. Without you, I would have no business, and every night I've fallen asleep imagining being able to repay you." He put some notes on the table, then he took a chequebook from his jacket pocket.

Mr Rossi frowned. "What is that for? The money will more than cover our breakfast."

Francesco ignored him. He wrote out a cheque, signed it and slid it across the table.

Mr Rossi looked at the amount on the cheque and blanched. "Oh no, no, no, I cannot take this."

"Your wife would want you to. This is so you can employ a physical therapist for Laura. In six months' time, I will send you another cheque."

Mr Rossi's eyes shone with tears.

"Consider it a debt repaid," Francesco said softly.

Chapter 9 – Majorca

William looked across the Club de Mar marina. A breeze blew in and filled the air with the soft clinking of halyards against the masts of the boats that sat in the marina, the cathedral watching over them from a distance. His heart lifted at the sight of the *Accidental Diamond*. Shearcourt was his home, but the Diamond was a fine, familiar place to be. A couple of deep, excited barks drifted across the marina and he grinned. He'd missed his dogs, and evidently, they'd missed him too.

He opened Grace's car door for her as Stephen unloaded their cases and took them over to the crew member waiting to take them aboard. As she stepped out into the sunshine, the sun caught her eyes for a moment and lit them a bright, amber-specked sea-glass green. For a moment, her delicate beauty made his stomach flutter.

She was looking up at him. "Palma is beautiful. The blue of the sky and the sea is stunning."

"Yes," William replied, "and thankfully, I have an old friend here who I hope may be able to help us in tracing our mysterious buyer."

"Another ex-army friend?" Grace asked.

"Sort of – Uwe is an ex-Austrian Army man. We met when we each served with our respective forces. He is providing us with a car. He'll pick us up for dinner at his house, and we can choose a car to use on the island."

"Is Stephen coming with us?"

"No, Uwe is someone I trust deeply. And whilst he is not a Society member, he has been a great friend to us at various times. Which means that we will be very safe with him, and Stephen can have a night off."

"What does Stephen do with his nights off?" Grace asked, her voice full of curiosity.

"Well, he has a family in Ireland, so he'll probably spend some time talking to them. Then reading military history books, I imagine."

"He seems very keen on military history."

"He's studying for a Master's degree," William said with a smile.

Grace laughed. "That man is fascinating."

***

Grace put down her laptop. She'd been researching organised crime in Majorca. The small, sunny island hid a sinister underworld in its shadows. The Majorcan Mafia were exceptionally well-connected. They were known to have links with the major crime families and organisations across Europe, from Kosovo to Sicily to Russia. The island even hosted conferences where the underworld leaders met, like a shadow G8 summit, to agree on areas of cooperation and define operations in and across their regions.

Grace looked out of the porthole of her cabin. The tranquil waters seemed so gentle and peaceful, yet Majorca was awash with corruption and crime. The Majorcan Mafia's operations extended into drugs, people- and weapons-trafficking, and of course, this required a substantial commitment to money laundering. And buying art, antiques and gemstones was an excellent way to clean dirty money.

Perhaps it was unsurprising that their path had brought them here. The Majorcan Mafia had the trade links and infrastructure to manage the smuggled gold in partnership with their neighbouring crime families.

But how were they moving so much gold without it coming to the attention of any authority?

When they'd last checked in, Gerrard had told her that he'd liaised with Interpol's head office and conducted his own review of the chatter on the Dark Web. There was a high volume of talk about the disruption to the old gold-smuggling routes but little intelligence about what the new ones were.

Whoever was behind this new route must have extensive access to transport, significant human resources and deep pockets to have invested in setting the route up so quickly.

She thought about the corruption investigations she'd conducted in prisons. Generally, a chance mistake, an unexpected change in routines in the prison or a disgruntled prisoner or staff member would be the catalyst in triggering an investigation into drug smuggling. Sometimes this initial thread would yield little beyond a corrupt officer or two, but sometimes it was the thread that unravelled a whole tapestry of unimaginable size. This would be the case here. They just needed to find that first thread – and they were close. She could feel it.

There was a knock at the door. Grace looked at her watch and frowned. She'd lost track of time. She needed to be ready for dinner in an hour. She stretched her sore shoulders and shouted, "Come in."

Hayley opened the door and entered, a garment bag folded over her arm. "I went into town to pick this up for you."

Grace raised an eyebrow. She'd packed the dresses from Dubai, but they were all quite formal, so she was curious to see what was in the bag.

"Thanks, Hayley." Grace took the bag and hung it up to unzip it.

"Oh, and Sarah had to return to her offices, but she asked me to give you this. She said you can keep this one." Hayley pulled a little box from her pocket and put it into

Grace's hand. "It's crew dinner now, so it'll be quiet up on deck. You can give me a call on my mobile if you need anything, though." Hayley smiled and turned to go.

"Enjoy your dinner."

Grace sat down on the bed and looked at the box. It was tied with ribbon and embossed with Sarah's company logo. There was a note slipped under the ribbon. Grace unfolded it and read.

"To Grace – the rising tide lifts all boats. I hope you like it. Sarah x."

She flipped the box open. Inside, a pretty gold necklace in the shape of a stylised yacht, embellished with a sapphire sea and a diamond star over the sails nestled against white satin.

She smiled and went to the mirror to put it on, making a mental note to get Sarah's office address from Hayley so she could send her a proper thank-you letter.

Grace turned her attention to the garment bag. Inside was a light, red floral dress with a neckline that left the tops of her shoulders bare, a well-fitted waist and a full skirt. It reminded her of a dress Brigitte Bardot might have worn in Monaco. It was just right for a meal on a sultry summer night.

***

William leaned against the railings and looked out across the sea. The sun was not yet starting to set, and the sky was filled with the golden iridescence of twilight.

Footsteps on the far side of the deck made him turn around. Grace had come up onto the deck. She looked breath-taking. The ruby tone of her dress suited her pale skin and dark hair well. She had not noticed him – from where she stood, the bar in the centre of the deck would obscure her view.

He was about to step towards her when he saw that she was holding her phone to her ear.

"No, Dave, I told you, really. I don't want you to wait, please... you should be out there looking for someone who will make you happy."

There was a silence as Grace listened to the reply.

"I'm sorry, I don't think talking about it will help. I just don't think we suit each other well. We're both good, nice people, but just not the ideal fit for each other. Anyway, I have to go. I have a work event tonight. OK, bye, Dave. You take care." She put the phone back in her bag and sighed.

William stepped forward. "I'm sorry, I was about to come and say hello when I realised you were on the phone."

"Oh, I... how much did you hear?"

"All of it."

Grace rolled her eyes. "Well, I'm sure the Society had already ascertained my relationship status."

William laughed. "Not beyond the bare facts that you are unmarried and don't have dependents, I promise you."

Grace smiled and shook her head.

"Are you OK?" William said, concern in his voice.

"Yes, fine, I just took the opportunity of working away to sever a tie at home that wasn't working well for either of us."

"And it sounds like 'Dave' is keen to maintain that tie."

"Yes. He's a good man. Sweet, kind, reliable, clever."

"He sounds like an excellent man. Why the need to sever the tie?"

Grace shrugged. "I just don't think we want the same things in life."

"Ah. I see. And what is it you want?"

"I'm not sure. But I'm pretty sure it's not being married to an accountant, living in a semi-detached house somewhere near London and working in the prison system until I get my pension."

"What did you want to do when you were a kid?"

"I wanted to be a geologist for a while, until I figured out that wasn't the same as getting to go around the world hunting for gems, but mostly I wanted to be a writer."

"What did you want to write? Fiction?"

"Yes, I've never really finished anything, but I'd love to write an adventure story of some sort. What did you want to do when you were a kid? Oh wait, you must already be doing it!" Grace finished with a giggle.

William threw his head back and laughed. "No, actually, I wanted to be a doctor, not an international playboy, but then the military called to me."

Grace looked at him gravely. "I'm sorry. I should stop stereotyping you as the archetypal rich, irresponsible ladies' man. It's not fair."

William spread his hands. "I understand. If I were in your shoes, I'd probably think the same about me." He turned to look out across the marina. "Well, Uwe will be here to collect us any minute," he said, his tone brisk.

Grace reached out and put her hand on his shoulder. "I'm serious, I'm sorry. I shouldn't have judged you like I did. I can see that you are more than that. The loyalty and respect that people around you have for you is mirrored in your loyalty and respect for them. I admire that."

William turned to face her. Her hand was still on his shoulder. He put out his hand as if to touch her cheek but instead turned the motion into a friendly pat on the arm.

"I appreciate that, thank you," he said, his voice quiet and his eyes soft as he looked down at her.

A cheerful beep-beep came from the marina.

A well-built man with dark hair cut close to his head, leaning against a black Range Rover, waved at them.

William waved back. "Let's go and introduce you to Uwe," he said, ushering her towards the walkway.

Uwe came forward and hugged William with great enthusiasm before kissing both of Grace's cheeks. His eyes crinkled when he smiled, and despite his imposing physique, he had an air of joviality and warmth about him.

They got into the car, and Uwe chatted amiably with William as they drove out of Palma into the mountains. The road was fringed with pine trees that trailed back to become forests gracing the rough-hewn lower slopes, and the early evening air was fresh with the scent of pine and the distant hint of orange blossom.

Uwe's house was at the end of a long, winding track – an old, traditional house with green shutters and flowering vines trailing all over the mellow stone walls.

A pretty blonde woman came to greet them.

"Jana, this is Grace," William said, as Jana bestowed kisses on their cheeks.

Uwe showed them through to a covered veranda. He poured them each an Aperol spritz, and they sat down to bread, olives and a selection of local cheeses.

"It has been too long, William," Uwe said.

"I agree, but it is lovely to see you and Jana again and to visit your beautiful home."

Jana beamed at him. "And it is so good that you have brought someone to meet us this time!" she said, taking Grace's hand and patting it.

Grace opened her mouth to say something, looking at William in confusion.

He smiled and nodded. "I am pleased to be able to introduce Grace to you both."

"The lamb will be ready shortly, but what do you say to a tour of the car I'm lending you? I think you will like it." Uwe grinned as he clapped William on the back.

"I can't wait," William said.

Uwe showed William and Grace over to a coach house on the far side of the house. A gleaming black car with smooth lines and a soft roof shone in the fading light.

"A Corvette Stingray!" William exclaimed. "She's exquisite. 1965? 66?"

"Close, 1967," Uwe confirmed.

Uwe started the Stingray and pulled her out into the courtyard. Her V8 engine burbled, a powerful idling growl that filled the air with the hot, rich smell of petrol.

William walked around it, taking in the shining wire wheels, tan leather interior and immaculate finish.

"We've just finished restoring her, so try not to ruin the paintwork," Uwe said with a grin.

"Thank you, Uwe, she's just what we need for our endeavour."

They walked back to the terrace.

"About that... I think I can get you a lunch reservation tomorrow," Uwe said.

"Oh really?" William said, looking sharply at Uwe.

"Yes, Mr Ramon Serra is willing to meet with you. It seems there is some curiosity about this big-money buyer at the auctions. He will probably be as keen to gain information from you as to give you information, but it is a start," Uwe said.

"How deeply involved with organised crime and corruption is Mr Serra?" Grace asked.

"He is second in command in one of the larger organisations operating from the island," Uwe said.

"Is there anything we need to be aware of from a security perspective?" Grace inquired.

"He had a reputation as having a slightly hot temper when he was younger, but he's smart and measured, on the whole. Here in Majorca, despite our issues with crime and corruption, these rarely spill over into violence. He's unlikely to be armed, although he is an established and well-trained fighter. He will have men with him as a show of power if nothing else, but I would not anticipate any difficulties, provided you engage with him respectfully," Uwe replied.

William nodded. "From what I understand, although the main crime groups here are deeply involved with international smuggling of all types, including that of guns, weapons and violence are rarely used openly on Majorca, unlike in Sicily, despite the close links the Majorcans have with their allies there. With diplomacy and good manners, I think we'll be safe enough. We'll take Stephen with us, however, just in case."

Grace inclined her head in agreement. "What are the exits like in the place we're meeting at?"

"Ramon suggested a traditional Majorcan restaurant in Cala Deia. I know it well. It is a good restaurant, right on the water, reached by a narrow track. There are open views out across the mountains, and most people favour a table on the open roof terrace. Now, this is both an advantage and a disadvantage. The terrace is reached by a narrow staircase. On the one hand, this means you only have one exit, which is easily blocked. However, you can mitigate that issue by ensuring that Stephen remains downstairs and monitors who comes in, checks the openness of your exit and provides backup if your exit is obstructed," Uwe said.

"I know the restaurant – we'll have Stephen sit downstairs at the front terrace, with a view into the restaurant of the staircase to the upper terrace," William replied.

"Perfect. And, of course, I also happen to be in Cala Deia tomorrow," Uwe said with a mischievous grin.

"Such a coincidence!" William replied, laughing. "Back to more important matters, did you say we have lamb for dinner? Is this your famous slow-cooked lamb?"

Uwe nodded. "It is the recipe that made Jana finally agree to marry me – and so I have cooked it every time I want to impress someone ever since."

"Uwe, I'm flattered. I've waited years for you to make me this dish," said William.

"Oh, it's not for you. Jana insisted that I make it because Grace was coming," Uwe replied with a wink.

***

Grace closed her eyes and tilted back her head. They had the soft top down on the Stingray. The sunlight warmed her skin, and the wind touched her hair with cool fingers. William glanced round at her. She was like a contented cat in a patch of sun, a smile curving her lips.

The road wound through the trees up into the mountains, scattered houses and villages of creamy stone dotted on the rugged slopes. One side of the road fell away to a sheer drop, with a valley tumbling down to the sea, which showed as a thin line of deep blue along a horizon blurred with the still dissipating morning mist.

Grace looked around. Stephen was following them in another of Uwe's cars – an old ex-military Land Rover Defender with a soft top and various tools and jerrycans strapped to the rear. She lifted her arm, waved at him, and saw him raise his hand in a salute. They were coming to a crossroads approaching a village, and William slowed the car.

As she started to turn in her seat, a large blue car appeared behind Stephen's. William looked in the mirror and made a hand signal to Stephen, who nodded.

Grace turned to William. "They're following us."

"We'll keep an eye on them. They've been on the road behind us for a while."

The blue car turned off at the crossroads. Grace breathed a sigh of relief.

The road narrowed to a tree-lined track. The tall pines threw shadows across their path, and Grace almost didn't see the blue car slewed across the street as they turned the corner for a moment. Three men stood around the car, waiting.

William slammed on the brakes, and they skidded to a stop. "Stay in the car. Get the tyre iron under your seat and keep it in your hand just in case," he said calmly.

Stephen pulled in behind them and left the car like a bullet, charging up the road towards them. William stepped out, and they faced the men. One was short and stocky, one older and scarred, and the third was young and muscular.

The short man, stocky, middle-aged with a hard face and lank hair, came forward. He looked Grace insolently up and down.

"Back off," William said, his voice a quiet, menacing growl.

The guy smirked and walked towards the car. "Pretty car. Pretty girl. Give me the car, and I might let you keep the girl," he sneered.

Stephen reached out, with surprising speed for a man of his size, grabbed the stocky man by the shirt, pulled him up to his face height and struck him with a swinging headbutt before throwing him back into the young one, who tumbled back into the car and fell to the ground. The older man piled forward towards William, who stepped aside and punched him hard in the gut. The man let out an "oof" of pain but recovered quickly and threw his weight onto William, taking him to the ground.

Feeling exposed in the open-top car, Grace crept out with the tyre iron held tightly against her chest, her heart pounding, and crawled around the car.

William was underneath the older man, who pulled back to punch him in the face. William shoved him back, deflecting the blow and creating enough room for him to lift his knee and strike it hard into his groin. The man yowled in pain and fell to the side. Still half underneath him, William pushed him away, but the man, recovering, tried to strike out at him again. William wrapped an arm against his neck, and they grappled on the ground.

Grace heard a yell of anger. The young one had picked himself up from the floor, where his companion still lay groaning and holding his face, reeling from the force of Stephen's headbutt, and, pulling a knife from his waistband, ran at Stephen.

Stephen deflected the young man's first strike with a heavy block using his forearm, which must have sent a shock down the man's arm, as the young man grunted in pain and surprise but quickly pushed forward again, raising the knife. Stephen fell back a little, making space between them, bringing the young man level with where Grace was hiding behind the car. Seeing him going to strike, she sprang up and hit him hard on the back of the head with the tyre iron. It made a sickening crack, and the man immediately crumpled like a puppet whose strings had been cut.

Stephen looked at her. "We'll talk about this later," he said curtly, then ran over towards William.

The older man struggled, then went limp. William let go of the man's neck, thrust him away and stood up. Stephen reached him, Grace following on his heels.

"Are you both OK?" William said, breathing heavily.

Grace looked down at the man lying motionless on the floor, the man groaning in a ball by the car and, turning, the silent young man prone, blood trickling from his scalp.

"More OK than they are," she said, her voice shaking a little. She'd seen plenty of incidents in the prisons, but as a civilian, your only job was usually to get out of the way. Sometimes a passing officer would shove you into the nearest cupboard, shouting at you to lock yourself in until the incident was over. She'd rarely seen violence and its aftermath at quite such close quarters. Her stomach felt chilled and her muscles were tight with adrenaline.

Stephen had lifted the young man easily and dumped him under the trees at the side of the road. He did the same with the other two, then started up their car and moved it so they could pass. As an afterthought, he took up the young man's knife from where he'd dropped it on the road and slashed their tyres before throwing the knife into the woods with a high arcing throw.

Grace stood looking at William. Somehow, she had not imagined him like this, brutal and fierce. He was usually so suave and polished that seeing him rolling on the floor brawling and choking someone out did not compute. She shook her head, dazed. Despite the day's warmth, her skin was covered in goose bumps.

William took off his jacket and draped it over her shoulders. His jacket smelt faintly of his cologne – a fresh, green chypre – and she felt comforted by his scent and the trace of warmth from his skin that the fabric still held.

He smoothed his hands down her arms, looking her over carefully before inspecting their car for damage.

Stephen came over to her. "Thanks for stepping in, although I assure you, I had him covered," he said, his voice crisp.

"He had a knife…." Grace said, looking imploringly at him.

Stephen softened. "Yes, he did. And to be clear, I would rather you stayed out of the way in any situation like that, but if you're going to insist on stepping in, we'll have to give you a bit of a personal safety training update."

Grace grinned. "OK." She hesitated for a moment. "Are they going to be alright?" She gestured towards the heap of prone and groaning men.

"All breathing. There'll be some bruises and sore bits for them tomorrow, but they'll live."

Grace let out a long breath. "Good." She walked back to the car. William started the Stingray up, and they continued on their way. The sun's warmth didn't quite quench the chill in her stomach, but the adrenaline-fuelled shaking of her muscles stilled a little as they headed back onto the narrow road, away from the blue car and its occupants.

***

William pulled up on a track under the trees, and they walked across an unpaved path along the edge of a beach to the restaurant. The restaurant sat above the water, with beautiful views across the sea. Stephen got out first and took a leisurely walk around the outside before taking a seat at the terrace at the front of the restaurant, directly opposite the stairs to the upper terrace. Three broad, serious-looking men sat at another table facing the stairs. They eyed Stephen, who looked stonily at them in return. These were Ramon Serra's men. A pretty waitress with long, dark hair and long-lashed golden eyes served them iced water and plates of sliced meats and cheese that the men ignored.

The owner of the restaurant greeted them, took William's jacket for him and ushered them up a set of steep stairs. The stairs opened out onto a small terrace built around two olive trees. Rattan was woven around through the trees to create a delightful space which looked out across the sparkling blue sea. There was only room for two tables. At one of them sat a lean, handsome man in his forties, his dark, slicked-back hair flecked with grey. He was wearing a pair of classic aviator sunglasses, gazing out to sea as they came up onto the terrace. He rose to his feet as William and Grace approached the table, offering William his hand and kissing Grace's cheek.

"Mr Serra," William said, his voice tightly controlled. His jaw was clenched and his eyes flinty.

"Ramon, please."

"Ramon. May I introduce Miss Grace Adair." William indicated to Grace.

"I am pleased to meet you," Ramon said. He studied William carefully. His manners were smooth, but his eyes were watchful. "I hope you had a pleasant journey."

William smiled wryly. "Unfortunately not. In fact, I rather wondered if you were aware of the difficulties we encountered on the road." He did not make it a question.

Ramon stared at him. "No, I am sorry to hear it. May I ask what happened?"

"We were attacked by a group of men who attempted to take the car," William said, meeting Ramon's eyes squarely. "I was concerned that they were, perhaps, somehow aware of our route."

"Are you implying, Mr Anderson, that I or my people had some involvement in your attack?" Ramon said, his voice quiet and dangerous.

William shrugged. "News travels fast on a small island."

Grace put her hand on William's arm. His muscles felt hard and tense under her fingers.

"It was a stressful situation, Ramon. The men insinuated that they may harm me too, which William and Stephen, our driver, did not relish, of course."

Ramon looked at her and frowned. "I am sorry that you had to experience this in my hometown. Rest assured that no man who formed part of our organisation would behave with such incivility."

Grace inclined her head. "It is not your fault that some opportunist took the chance to try to take a handsome car in a secluded spot on the road."

William's muscles flexed under her touch. She squeezed his arm.

"I apologise, Ramon. Let us take our seats. I have been told that this restaurant serves the finest lobster stew. I am keen to try it."

Ramon's face remained stony and impassive, but he smiled and gestured to the table. "And the view is unparalleled."

"I did not see many cars on the track," William remarked. "Did you arrive by boat?"

"Yes," Ramon replied, "it is such a fine day. It was a pleasure to be out on the sea."

They sat down. Their host returned with menus and a tray laden with platters of local cheeses, cured meats, bowls of olives, almonds and tapenade.

"I took the liberty of bringing a bottle of my own wine for us," Ramon said.

The host poured glasses for them. The wine was a rich golden colour that glowed in the sunlight.

William swirled his wine, took in the scent and sipped at it. "Beautiful. Silky, full of the flavour of ripe fruit, yet acidic. This will be delicious with seafood."

Ramon nodded. "The Malvasia grapes are hand-picked from our vines, some of the oldest in the region. I am, of course, biased, but it holds all of the flavours of home for me."

Grace took a sip of her wine and leaned back in her seat with a sigh.

Ramon smiled sympathetically. "I think you deserve some wine after such a tense journey," he said, his voice softening as he spoke.

Grace smiled in return. "It was not the start to our day that we wanted, but at least we arrived in one piece. And now the adrenaline is wearing off, I find myself profoundly hungry." She added slices of cheese and a spoonful of tapenade to her plate.

***

The tension around the table felt less palpable, although William noticed that Ramon remained watchful and somewhat cool when he spoke to him. He cursed himself inwardly. He had let his anger about the attempted car theft and the subsequent threats and violence cloud his judgement. It had been discourteous of him to accuse Ramon of setting up the incident. Even if he were involved, there was nothing to be gained by confronting him like this. William was thankful that Grace had defused the growing heat between him and Ramon with her gentle, delicate redirection.

Their lobster stew arrived, a local speciality made with the light red lobsters that flourished around Majorca, cooked with tomatoes, peppers, onions and fresh parsley. A basket of rustic bread and a dish of smooth, garlicky aioli completed the meal perfectly.

A moist almond cake flavoured with cinnamon and lemon zest arrived with coffee and they chatted amicably over their dessert.

William paused with his coffee cup in his hand. It would have been rude to rush the business. They were all well aware what they were meeting to discuss, but now the plates were cleared from the table, he needed to drive the conversation on.

"When we were in Dubai, we heard that a new face was buying up diamonds and gemstones across the major auction houses in Europe," he said. "I know that you are a keen collector yourself. Do you have any idea who the mysterious buyer might be?" he continued, sipping his coffee casually.

Ramon shrugged. "I wish I did. We are all rather curious about where this buyer is getting his money. It has attracted attention here, too."

"We did hear that one of the men sent to act on this buyer's behalf had links to Majorca," William said.

Ramon leaned back in his chair and looked at him. "Not one of ours." He waved his hand airily.

"I see," William said.

"We are all curious about this buyer, naturally, because buying up pieces like that would indicate someone who is moving money in a way that may encroach on interests of our own, so we would be keen to hear the results of your probing, but sadly we have nothing we can offer you at this time," Ramon said. His tone was cordial and somewhat apologetic, but his eyes were cold and hard.

"Of course," William said, bowing his head slightly in a respectful gesture. "Well, thank you for a beautiful lunch. The food was excellent, and we appreciate your time." He rose. The host had already brought his jacket, which he took, paying his compliments to the chef.

Grace stood too. "Thank you for your hospitality."

Ramon leaned forward and kissed her cheeks.

"*Bona tarda.*" He shook William's hand, then turned and walked down the stairs ahead of them. They followed. Stephen was standing as they reached the final steps, as were Ramon's men.

The waitress stood watchfully near the door. She met Grace's eye for a moment, her gaze steady and sharp before she dropped her eyes and respectfully stepped back as they passed.

Ramon strode off, towards the water, without looking back, his men following.

William walked back along the track to the car with Grace, Stephen keeping close behind.

"Dead end," he said.

Grace nodded. "I got a sense that Ramon and his boss were keener to find out what we knew than to communicate anything to us."

"I got that impression too."

Chapter 10 – A Gift Rewarded

Brescia, Italy, 1987

Francesco stood looking at Laura. She was radiant, her sweet face lit with delight.

"When?" Francesco asked, emotion choking his voice as he hugged her to his chest.

"Around Christmas. Won't that be beautiful, a Christmas baby!" She danced in his arms.

"Have you told your papa?" Francesco said, grinning wildly, his heart thumping hard as he held her to him.

"Not yet," Laura said, "and I am hoping he does not think too hard on the dates," she said with a giggle.

Francesco laughed. "I don't think he will. We are married now. After all, that is all that matters. Besides, he will be so happy to be a grandfather that I don't think he'll care to mention it."

"I think you are right," Laura agreed. "I cannot wait to tell him!"

She snuggled into Francesco's arms, putting her hands into his pockets. He felt her fingers touch the shell he still kept with him.

"You've never told me why you keep this shell in your pocket," she said, beaming up at him.

He closed his eyes for a moment. "When I was a little boy, I always wanted to go to the beach, but we never managed to go. I traded some lost marbles I'd collected from the playground for the shell. It was my first trade. It made me so happy to hear the sound of the sea when I held it to my ear. I keep it to remind me that every avalanche starts with a single snowflake and that I can build a world if I put my mind to it, brick by brick."

Laura squeezed him. "Let's go to the beach whenever we can, Francesco."

He held her close to his heart. His mind was already on how he could expand the businesses, buy up some further factories and increase their production. He would move into trading scrap metals. There was good money in that. He would have a child to provide for.

He thought of his own father. Antonio Castelli had vanished, drink having robbed him of what decency he had as a father and a husband. That was not him. He would provide for Laura and their baby – and who knew, maybe they would have more babies! They would want for nothing.

After he had given Mr Rossi the money for Laura's physical therapy, she had made an excellent recovery. When she had been able to walk, she'd insisted on walking to the factory on her own to thank him.

Francesco smiled at the memory.

She'd walked into his factory carrying an *uva fragola* cake – filled with the fragrant, lush Lombardy-grown grapes that he adored, and as he watched her move through the factory floor towards him like a ray of sunshine, she stole his heart.

He considered himself in Mr Rossi's debt. He had helped him once, and Francesco had tried to pay him back, but in introducing him to his daughter, Mr Rossi had given him a gift that could not be repaid.

Laura dropped a kiss against his neck and wriggled free, heading for the telephone to invite her father for dinner.

She was, Francesco thought, the very pulse of his heart.

***

Francesco had driven back from the hospital as if he was transporting a cargo of rare porcelains.

The baby had Laura's dark curls. He touched one of the tiny coils with his forefinger. He didn't know if he'd ever felt anything softer. Rosa reached out and gripped his finger with her little hand.

Laura smiled up at him. "You're never going to be able to say no to her, are you? The battle is already lost. It took her all of a day to conquer your heart." Her eyes twinkled mischievously.

"She must get it from her mama." Francesco grinned.

Laura rocked the baby in her arms. She lifted her head, tears suddenly in her eyes.

Francesco frowned in concern. "What is wrong, Laura?"

She smiled, making the tears spill over and trickle down her cheeks. Francesco smoothed them with his fingers, waiting for her to speak.

"Nothing is wrong. It is just… so overwhelming. This little baby, our little Rosa, will be a grown woman one day. Maybe she'll have a daughter of her own. We have a child, Francesco, a person we're responsible for!" She gave a hiccupping laugh through her tears.

Francesco felt his own eyes sting. "I know. I could not be luckier. I'll move heaven and earth for my girls. Whatever she needs, whatever you need, whatever it takes to make you happy."

He bent down to kiss Laura, her face damp and salty from her tears.

A knock at the door made them both jump. The baby stirred and began to cry.

"You get the door. I'll take her into the nursery. I think she might need changing," she said, turning to go.

Francesco nodded and went to the door. "Carlo!" Francesco clapped his hand on the man's shoulder in surprise and delight.

"I heard you have a new addition to the family!" Carlo still had the same infectious grin.

He held out a large box wrapped in pink satin ribbon. "Congratulations."

"It's been so long." Francesco gestured for Carlo to come in. "Tell me how you are, how is business, the family?"

"Well, I never married Sophia Loren's sister, but I did find a wife almost as beautiful."

Francesco paused. He had heard that Carlo had married the daughter of a businessman strongly suspected of having connections with the Mafia.

"Congratulations. I hope you are enjoying married life."

"Life is good, business is good. I'm working for my father-in-law." Carlo grinned.

Laura came back into the room, holding Rosa.

"Carlo, this is my wife Laura and our baby Rosa."

Carlo kissed Laura on each cheek and fussed over Rosa, stroking her tiny fingers gently.

"Beautiful, Franco, you are truly blessed," he said.

Laura put the baby into Francesco's arms while she went to make coffee.

"I hear your businesses are growing well," Carlos said as he sat down.

"Yes, we have both come a long way." Francesco smiled.

"We always said we would."

"We did."

Laura returned with the coffee. Carlo took photos of his wife from his wallet, and they swapped news and talked until the baby began to cry again.

"I should go, but it has been a pleasure to see you. Let's not leave it so long next time." Carlo shook hands with Francesco and kissed Laura goodbye. "If you can find the time, it would be good to meet for dinner one day, Franco. I have a business proposal for you."

"Of course. Give our best wishes to your wife. We hope to meet her someday soon," Francesco replied.

They watched him get into his shiny sports car and drive off.

Laura gave Francesco a long look as he shut the door.

"I'd rather you didn't get into business with him, Francesco," she said seriously. "Do you know who his father-in-law is?"

Francesco nodded. "I do – and yes, I've never had any desire to get into business with Carlo. He is fun and a kind man in his own way, but his fondness for money has always led him down dubious paths."

"You've worked hard for what you have. There's no need to go down those paths."

"I agree. I have too much to lose. And besides, I'd never hear the last of it from you, would I?" he said with a laugh.

"Oh no, you would not. And just for mentioning it, you're on baby-changing duty for the rest of the day."

Francesco rolled his eyes in mock annoyance. Laura smiled and ran her fingers through his hair.

He pulled her close to him, Rosa nestled between them.

Chapter 11 – The Reverse Pickpocket

William walked up onto the deck and stopped, watching the scene in front of him with interest.

Grace dodged Stephen's fist.

"Good!" Stephen said. "Now block."

Grace brought her forearm up to deflect Stephen's hand as it came towards her in a fast slap, moving away from him and following up with a kick toward his groin. "Can I ask a question?" Grace said, panting a little.

"Sure."

"You know when those guys went for the car – why did you pick up the mouthy one and headbutt him? Headbutting seems a high-risk way to start a fight."

Stephen laughed. "Did they teach you about primary attack strategies in your SPEAR training?"

Grace nodded.

"Well, only Scotland, England and Ireland consider a headbutt a good way to start a fight. Most other countries don't consider it an opening move. That goes to our advantage in a situation such as yesterday. People don't expect it – it has shock value. It sends a very clear message that you are fully committed to not taking any crap and amps up the intimidation to the extent that it will sometimes send any other opponents running," Stephen said casually.

"I wouldn't recommend it as a useful move for someone of your stature unless you are in a situation where you can throw your head back into someone's nose if they have you pinned. Remember what we said? If you can't de-escalate or run away, go for the bits that cause the most pain. Now, what do we do for a bear hug?" He stepped behind Grace and locked his arms around her chest, pinning her arms to her sides.

***

Paws clattered on the deck as the confused dogs came running up to join Stephen and Grace. Morrigan stood in front of Grace, barking and wagging her tail, unsure if they were playing or not.

"Sit, Morrigan." William's voice was calm but aloof.

Grace looked up. Her face was flushed from the exercise. Stephen had his arms around her.

William's heart contracted.

"Thank you, Stephen. I believe I can take it from here," he said tersely.

Stephen gave him a measured look, a smile creasing the corner of his mouth, then released Grace and stepped away.

"You did well today," he said, giving her a high five and walking off towards the kitchens.

Grace was frowning at William. "We were halfway through training," she said, hands on her hips.

William smiled. "I would rather train you myself. Stephen's height and build mean he does not always appreciate the adaptations necessary for those who cannot rely on their height and weight in a fight."

"You're six foot three and built like Thor," Grace said.

"Yes, but if you recall, I have a mother and sisters – and I have trained all of them in self-defence."

Grace narrowed her eyes. "I rather think I should be able to choose who trains me," she snapped.

"I don't know what gave you that impression," William said. He regretted the words as soon as they left his mouth.

Grace compressed her lips and looked away, refusing to meet his eye.

"Training in personal safety is usually decided around the best fit between trainer and trainee," he said, trying to repair the damage, "on the basis of previous experience, training style and how well the disciplines the trainer teaches fit the student."

"Right. Not due to your own personal preferences," Grace said.

"No. Not due to my personal preferences," William agreed. Although he imagined that both Stephen and Grace suspected his motivation for wanting to train Grace himself. The strength of his feelings for her had taken him by surprise. He really liked this clever, elegant and resilient woman. "We'll start training tomorrow," he said.

"No. I was halfway through a session. You owe me half a session," Grace said. She threw her hand out in a palm strike aimed at his chest. He caught her wrist easily and pulled her in towards him into a bear hug.

As he drew her against his chest William felt an unfamiliar crinkle within his jacket.

He frowned, gently took his hands from Grace's arms and let her go.

"What?" she said, surprised at his sudden disengagement.

"There's something in my jacket pocket." Reaching into the inner pocket, he drew out an envelope. "I did not put that in my pocket."

"The host took your jacket in the restaurant. There was ample opportunity to tamper with it," said Grace.

They stood looking at it. It was a simple manila envelope, unsealed and folded in half.

"Do you think it contains anything noxious?" Grace said.

"No, I think it would be sealed if it had any kind of powder in it." William reached into his breast pocket and pulled out a handkerchief then carefully opened the envelope and looked inside. A slip of paper sat in the folds of brown paper. Even without taking it out, the words were visible.

"Geneva Freeport," he read.

"Ha," Grace snorted. "A classic prison-style tip-off note. Favoured by those who don't want to be seen as a grass but do want to pass on information to take out someone inconvenient."

"Do you think it's credible?" William raised an eyebrow.

She thought for a moment. "I'd say so, yes. The Majorcans have an interest in ensuring we limit the activities of a potential rival."

William rubbed his chin. "Yes, even if they are working with our gold smuggler presently, it might suit them to take him out of play and leave a gap in the market they could fill, now they know how. Well, well, Ramon. Such double-dealing. Shall we take the bait, Grace?"

"Let's do it."

***

The meeting had progressed at a fast pace. William glanced down at his notebook. It was filled with a scrawl of notes and ideas to chase up later. Grace shifted on the sofa next to him, leaning forward, focused on Amira and Gerrard's faces on the big screen.

"There are several companies and individuals who have the manufacturing, metalworking and trade links to be able to melt down gold and move it," Amira said. "I listed the assets, company infrastructure and facilities required to engage in this sort of work. Gerrard and his team have traced all of the potential parties across Europe who may be able to facilitate gold smuggling at this scale."

Gerrard shared his screen to show a list of companies. "We discounted a number of them as unlikely to have the connections and reach to build relationships with the gold smugglers and with those people interested in buying untraceable gold in Europe – who will primarily be underworld figures," he said.

William looked at the list. There were ten companies, mainly in Tunisia, Germany and Italy.

"Germany seems unlikely, although we should not discount the German companies. Tunisia or Italy seem more likely, due to the greater prevalence of corruption and more established links with organised crime," William said.

"Can we cross-check those Italian companies to establish which of them have existing interests in Africa and if any of the owners and executives are known to have an interest in trading fine jewels?" Grace suggested.

Gerrard nodded. "I'll get on it."

"I am looking into ensuring we have the means to rapidly analyse any samples of gold we are able to get hold of if we can make inroads into the smuggling gang and capture some gold before it is re-smelted," Amira said.

"Gerrard, can you start looking at the Freeport in Geneva to establish if there is any increased activity from Africa, Tunisia or Italy? The Freeport would make an ideal hub to wash money from the gold-smuggling route, so if we can compare the leads we have for companies potentially involved with shipments going into the Freeport, we may get somewhere," William said.

"We'll fly to Geneva tomorrow. I have a contact there who may be willing to give us some intelligence. The activities within the Freeport are strictly confidential and very difficult to establish. Still, we may be able to use our inside man to identify relevant accounts with increased activity," he continued.

They said their goodbyes and ended the call.

"Right," William said with a grin. "I believe I owe you a training session."

***

Grace walked out onto the main deck. The sea shone under a bright Mediterranean sun and cloudless sky. It was still early and not yet hot, but the day held the promise of long, warm hours on deck with a book.

William was waiting by the railings, looking out across the water. She'd never seen him out of tailored clothing before. In his simple, well-fitting white T-shirt and joggers, there was no missing the powerful muscles of his tall frame. Without the civilising influence of a suit, he looked plain dangerous – and distractingly masculine.

The dogs were sleeping peacefully by his feet, in a tumble of limbs. Aurora opened one eye as Grace approached, snuggled her head back against her sister's flank and went back to sleep. Grace smiled at them. Their silver fur glistened and their sleek frames, even in sleep, held a clear strength. She could see why William had chosen them. They suited him well.

"I take them everywhere if I can," William said, seeing her look at the dogs. "They like being aboard the Diamond. There are lots of smells to enjoy, the crew love to play with them and Chef likes to spoil them with scraps of meat."

Grace laughed. "They have a good life. They must enjoy being at your house in Ireland, too."

William nodded. "Yes, they do, very much. But there they work more and get spoiled less, so I think they are happy to get an occasional holiday."

William looked down at her. Although Stephen was taller than William, there was a quiet, elegant power in William's movements that always made her conscious of his presence.

"Ready to train?" He indicated to the bag of kit on the deck.

"Yes, although I'm not sure you're ready for me," Grace said with a wink. "Stephen says I have a much stronger punch than I look like I should have."

"Duly noted," William replied with a grin. "What did you and Stephen work through?"

"Grabs to the neck with one and two hands, bear hugs from behind, 360 defences, palm strikes, hammer fists…" Grace thought for a moment "…and groin kicks."

"OK, great start. What are you most concerned about in the type of situation we found ourselves in the other day?"

"Well, if one of those guys had grabbed me, I'd be worried about them getting me into a bear hug, but I have a better sense of how to deal with that now. If I couldn't de-escalate or run away, my main concern would be being taken to the ground. I'm worried my small size would be a real disadvantage," she said.

William's eyes crinkled with his smile of approval. "Well observed. Yes, being on the floor is an exceptionally vulnerable position to be in. We'll work on break-falls, getting back up, if you can, and then we'll look at getting out of difficult situations on the floor if you can't."

He pulled a couple of mats from a store at the side of the deck and lined them up to create a training space, demonstrated a break-fall and lay explaining the technique to Grace from the floor.

With a sudden surge of mischievousness, she sprang on him and pinned him flat, with her knees pressed against his biceps and the palm of her hand on his forehead.

"They taught us this in first aid," she said, grinning. "If you are checking if someone is breathing, keep your hand on their forehead, and your arm braced. It is very hard for them to sit up or move if you have control of their head like that."

William snorted. "And did they tell you what to do when you inevitably can't keep that up against a large, angry opponent?"

Grace opened her mouth to reply, but her words turned to an "oof" of expelled breath as William flexed his arms, flipped her off him and onto her back and landed smoothly over her, pinning her to the ground.

She giggled, the movement of her chest as she laughed pressing her against him. She looked up at him. There was laughter in his eyes too, but her breath caught as he held her gently but unshakeably to the mat.

She looked away, flushing, and the moment was broken.

Chapter 12 – Her Sun Set Whilst It Was Yet Day

Brescia, Italy, 1990

Mr Rossi stood over Francesco. He was crouched on the floor in the hospital car park, his arms wrapped around his head as if shielding himself from blows, his finely cut suit crumpled and his hair wild from running his despairing fingers through it again and again. He looked very much like the hungry, haunted-eyed little boy he'd seen outside the factory all those years ago.

His heart contracted with grief, for Laura, for the baby, for his wife and for Francesco. So much loss. His own knees felt weak with the weight of it, and he crumpled down on the kerb next to Francesco, his arm around the younger man's shoulders.

They sat in silence. The silence rolled on and on, pressing in on them. There was nothing to say. Laura and Rosa, their little girl, had been severely injured when a truck hit them head-on on a narrow road as she drove them home from a picnic in the mountains. They had no chance of survival. The hospital had merely been able to ease their suffering in the short hours they had left.

The doctors and nurses had tried, he knew, but everyone in the hospital, from the medical staff to the priest, had looked on helplessly as Laura and her little one slipped away from them whilst Francesco sobbed by their bed. He, too, had looked on, filled with the horror not only of his own loss but of Francesco's. He, at least, had the privilege of seeing his Laura grow up, seeing her find love, seeing her have a child of her own. Francesco would not get to see Rosa grow up. It was unbearable.

Slowly, Mr Rossi pulled Francesco to his feet. He came with him, quiet and docile as if he were sleepwalking. He looked at Francesco's car. Francesco was not in a fit state to drive, and neither was he. He took Francesco's arm and guided him through the streets to his mother's house.

The bustling streets in the spring sunshine was alien. The laughter of children rang out from the park as they passed by and it felt like an insult to their grief. He was nonsensically angry at the sound of their joy. He glanced at Francesco. He didn't appear to have heard them. He put one foot in front of the other slowly, deliberately, seeming not to care where he went beyond that one step.

Mrs Castelli opened the door with a smile that faded when she saw Francesco's grey, broken face. She glanced at Mr Rossi.

"What happened?" she said quietly.

Still, Francesco didn't stir, didn't look up. He was like a statue, frozen in his shock and grief.

Mr Rossi shook his head. His own face crumpled as he tried to frame the words.

Paling, Mrs Castelli took Francesco's hand and took him inside. She led him to the sofa, where he sat, obediently, when told to.

She drew Mr Rossi into the kitchen. He closed his eyes. To communicate the loss to Mrs Castelli was almost more than he could bear. His mouth dried as he tried to speak.

***

Francesco opened his eyes. He was lying on the bed he had slept in as a child. He couldn't tell how long he'd been there. Hours, days, he didn't know. He was still wearing his clothes, although his mother had slipped off his shoes and jacket.

He gazed unseeing at the same ceiling he'd looked at for all those years. He'd tried to persuade his mother to let him buy her a new place, somewhere out of the city, with a pretty garden, but she wouldn't let him, so he'd bought this house for her.

He reached into his pocket and took out his shell. He turned it over and over in his fingers and held it to his ear. It gave its familiar seashore whoosh – the sound of his own blood flowing through his body, he now knew, of course, rather than the ghost of the waves he'd thought it to be when he was a boy. He was glad he could hear the sound. He wasn't sure how else he would know he was alive. He felt nothing. Nothing at all. He was almost curious about his numbness, the same way he had been when the doctor had given him a local anaesthetic to sew up a gash in his leg when he'd fallen as a child. He'd poked at the flesh, marvelling at how it remained part of him, but incapable of sensation.

He looked again at the shell between his fingers. A spasm of anger shook him. This, this was all he had left. He clenched it hard in his fist. With a burst of remorse, he opened his hand and looked at it, checking in case he had crushed it. It sat on his palm, smooth and perfect

This little shell, his first trade – he'd built an empire, one piece at a time after that. This was all he had. Business. Trading. That was all that was left. No one could take that from him. He'd build his business day and night.

Chapter 13 – Palma to Geneva

William gazed out of the window. The plane had started its steep descent. Geneva was spread out below them, the lake shimmering in the sunshine and the green of the countryside pushing against the edges of the city. He looked over. Grace slept in the seat opposite him. The air conditioning had brought goose bumps to her skin, and William had gently tucked his soft, finely knit merino pullover across her bare arms. She'd stretched out her bare feet in her sleep and folded them between his own. He felt the warmth of her skin against him. He resisted the urge to reach down and stroke the tender skin on the inside of her ankle. It troubled him how much he wanted to touch her, to be in her company, to talk to her, to sit quietly with her – just to be with her.

They had business to conduct, and Grace had made it clear that she saw him as a pleasure-seeking womaniser. He couldn't deny there had been some truth to that in the past – he had leaned into the façade over the years, but not now. Now, he disliked the superficiality of casual affairs, wanting something of more substance. But how would that work with Grace? She had a career and a home in London. She wouldn't want to be trailing around the world with him, and she definitely wouldn't want to deal with not seeing him for months at a time. He'd seen how that worked out for military men away from home – it was a challenge for most and often didn't end well, with many relationships crumbling under the pressures of distance and time apart.

The plane's descent woke Grace. She stretched sleepily and snuggled against his pullover for a moment before opening her eyes. Realising she'd put her feet between his, she hastily drew them back with a mumbled apology and a blush rising in her cheeks. She ran her fingers over the soft knit, folding it and handing it back to him.

"What are the timings for the rest of our day?" she said.

"We'll collect a car at the airport and drive to my house. The chef has come over from the Diamond, so we'll have dinner there and analyse the briefing Amira and Gerrard have prepared for us. Tomorrow morning, we will go riding with Yannick, my contact at the Freeport."

"Riding?" Grace said.

"Yes, you can ride, can't you? You seemed to know rather a lot about the Household Cavalry," William said, a small smile playing at the edge of his mouth.

Grace laughed. "That was because our elderly neighbour, who I was very fond of, was a military history enthusiast. I can ride, but I haven't ridden for years, not since I was a young girl, really."

"Well, it will come back to you in no time at all."

"I haven't got riding gear with me," Grace said.

"You know what I'll say to that, don't you?" William grinned.

"Don't tell me. Correctly sized boots, breeches and a riding helmet will be in my wardrobe on arrival," she said, her face deadpan.

"Employers are obliged to supply personal protective equipment and clothing appropriate to the tasks their employees are required to fulfil in the course of their duties," he said in a mock-serious tone. "And there's also a pair of leather chaps."

"Firstly, I'm not sure how Harry Winston diamonds and Valentino dresses qualify as personal protective clothing, and secondly, I believe I'm employed by Her Majesty's Prison Service."

"I will acknowledge that you are not, technically, my employee but would point out that diamonds and couture are, in fact, protective clothing in the context of our present mission," William said.

Grace laughed. "Fine. Given that you generously concede that I am not your employee, I will generously concede that you are right. It is important to have the correct wardrobe for the occasion."

"And you are so elegant. You look like you were born to wear fine things," William said.

Grace looked as if she was going to make a wry comment in reply, but his earnest expression must have stopped her.

"Very far from that, Mr Anderson," she said. She turned her face away from him and looked out of the window. They were coming in to land.

***

Stephen opened the door of the waiting Bentley for Grace. She slid into the car and looked around. The seats were a butter-soft creamy leather, and light, glossy walnut accented the interior. William took a seat in the back with Grace.

Stephen headed out of the airport and drove them smoothly through the early evening traffic. The cars thinned as they reached the outskirts of the city, and the road opened out to fields dotted with wooden shuttered houses, cheerful pots of flowers around their doors. They drove along the edge of the lake, and Grace studied the placid waters with their elegant sailboats and regal yachts with interest.

The car pulled into a long driveway and drew up in front of a large, angular, brutally solid yet elegant house built of concrete, black steel and wood.

William showed Grace into the house. The dogs, who had travelled over with the chef, came running to greet them, tails wagging furiously with excitement. Morrigan sat next to William's legs and leaned her great head against him, waiting to be petted. Aurora nudged at Grace's hands, and she caressed the soft, velvet ears and rubbed her head.

Floor-to-ceiling windows in the main living area looked out onto the lake. The evening sun flooded the room, which was clad in wood, with the same black steel contrasting against the warm tones of the panelling. It was a stunning room. Somehow, despite the grand pro-portions, it managed to be cosy and inviting, with a modern metal stove to one side and an assortment of leather couches and chairs arranged around the fireplace. The stove was lit, flames dancing cheerfully. Grace walked over to warm her hands. The spring evening was chilly, despite the golden sunshine that the day had offered.

"This is a beautiful house," she said as William came over to join her.

"Thank you. I don't have the opportunity to stay here often, but it's useful for business – and the staff and crew like to use it for holidays with their families."

Grace inclined her head. "I would have thought it was expensive for them to hire."

"They can hire it for just the cost of cleaning the house and washing the linen," William said. "One of the perks of the job. We take good care of our people. They are our family, and their families are our own."

"Is this your house, or does it belong to the Moonlight Society?"

"Mine – but the Moonlight Society contributes towards maintenance so that we can offer the house for staff vacations."

"How is the Society funded? Government?"

"No, there were several legacies from founder members which have subsequently been invested and grown. The holdings and assets of the Society are, at this time, extensive."

Grace nodded. "They must be. The *Accidental Diamond* alone must cost a huge amount to maintain."

"Indeed, although it is cheaper and more adaptable than our former central London headquarters," William said, taking a seat in one of the wingback armchairs. He invited Grace to take a seat on the other, next to the fire.

They sat in companionable silence, listening to the crackling of the fire and looking out at the lake for a while. The dogs tumbled on the rug, basking in the stove's warmth.

William rose and filled crystal glasses with whiskey. He put them on the table between their chairs, together with the bottle.

Grace picked up the bottle and inspected the label. "Hinch eighteen-year-old single malt Château De La Ligne cask-finished whiskey. This sounds like a special whiskey."

"The distillery is on the estate of an old friend," William replied, lifting his glass and holding it to the light. The whiskey shone a deep gold.

Grace swirled the whiskey. The scent of freshly turned summer earth and ripe fruit rose from the glass, warm and comforting.

William pressed some controls, and music drifted softly to her ears. Nina Simone, she thought. She leaned back in her chair and closed her eyes. "Sinnerman." She smiled. How apt.

"How did you come to be working in a prison?" he asked, stretching out to pass a box of chocolate almonds to her.

She nibbled one. "I always wanted to help people. I didn't intend to get into forensic work at first, but that's where my road took me. I started out working in youth clubs. The kids I wanted to work with were the naughty ones who weren't allowed in, so I went to work with the youth offending service. Next thing you know, we're fifteen years or so down the line and forensic work is my specialism."

"Funny how things shape up. I could place a bet that investigating international gold smuggling wasn't on your to-do list." William smiled.

"No, it wasn't." She laughed. "But I'm glad I'm here."

"I'm glad you're here too."

They were quiet. The crackle of the fire and the snores of the dogs filled the silence they left.

"So, who's joining us for dinner?" Grace said at last.

"Just us. Stephen has gone to visit some friends, and Chef declined my invitation to join us in favour of a sports match on TV," he replied casually.

"Oh," Grace said. She tried to keep her voice neutral, but the thought of spending the evening alone with William was daunting. It was hard to escape his charm, the intense masculinity of his presence and his disarming humour and gentleness when they were alone. She tried to remind herself that he probably had half a dozen girlfriends around the world and that she was here to work, but the longer she spent with him, the more she saw there was more to this man than the superficially lavish and expensive lifestyle. She shook her head. She needed to keep her mind on their project. Soon she would be back in London, facing the daily commute to the prison with its tall, forbidding, cold walls, in her flat, listening to the distant roar of the traffic. That was her life and her reality. This was just an interlude. It could never be anything more.

***

William opened his eyes, rolled over and ran his hand over the cold, empty pillow beside him. He sighed. Grace had been in his dreams, and the space in his bed was an unwelcome reminder of her absence. She might never be in his bed, he reminded himself firmly. He tried to move his feet but found that they were heavily weighted by both Morrigan and Aurora, who had squeezed themselves along

111

his feet and legs. He grinned. They were not allowed on the bed, but he found it hard to be strict with them when they looked so happy to be lying at his feet, and besides, at least someone was sharing his bed, he thought.

It had been a pleasant dinner the night before. After going through their briefing documents from Amira and Gerrard, they sat long after their meal talking and laughing. They'd sat out on the deck next to the water, with the heaters blazing and blankets wrapped around them. They'd sat close enough to touch. But they hadn't touched.

He got up and walked into his bathroom to take a shower, hoping to wash the heat from his mind and body.

In the kitchen, Grace sat at the breakfast bar with Stephen and Chef. William took a seat with them.

Grace was dressed in the breeches, polo shirt and short boots with chaps that had awaited her in the closet and her hair was tied in a neat bun at the nape of her neck. A riding jacket was slung on the back of her chair. She looked fresh and chic, and her face shone with happiness as she talked with Stephen. William felt a twinge of sadness. He wanted her to look like that all the time. When he'd seen her in the governor's office, she'd looked austere, reserved and buttoned-up. Constrained by her surroundings and her role. He loved to see her looking free and joyful.

"How do you know Yannick?" Grace asked as William joined them.

"Yannick has trained horses for us at various points here and in Ireland, and we ride together whenever we can. He has a military background, and we like to talk about our regiments. But, most importantly for today's purposes, he has close connections with the Freeport," William said.

"Amira has sent through some further information about our shortlist of companies. If Yannick can help us to identify accounts with increased activity utilising the Freeport, we can cross-reference these with our shortlist and with luck, we may find ourselves a solid lead."

"But we have to go riding first?" Grace asked, her face full of mischief.

William shrugged. "It would be rude to get straight to business – and besides, it's a solid cover story for our visit to Yannick."

"I think I'm beginning to understand the diplomacy and etiquette of your circles."

They finished breakfast and headed out, their route following the shore of the lake. There were scattered houses along the serene road, behind grey stone walls. The countryside was a fresh green, and the spring air was clean and crisp. The distant mountains were tipped with white, and William detected a hint of the scent of snow in the breeze.

The gate to Yannick's drive swung open at their arrival, and they drove up the long picket-fenced approach, through grazing fields, past a sand arena, a covered manège and the livery yard, to the house. Yannick's home was a handsome old building. It had rambling wings and additions, opening to a wide porch, flanked by rows of windows shuttered with sun-bleached wood.

A handsome man with close-cropped dark hair jogged down from the porch to meet their car. He was dressed for riding, and his quietly expensive clothing showed off his athletic frame. He clapped William on the shoulder and pulled him into a hug as he got out of the car before doing the same to Stephen. As William introduced her, he bestowed a kiss on each of Grace's cheeks with a warm welcome.

Yannick showed them to a sunny table on the terrace, looking out towards the mountains, with a pot of coffee waiting for them, before they headed out to ride.

"You must be rusty, my old friend. With all of this sailing you are doing, you must barely catch sight of a horse from one month to the next," Yannick said, with a glint in his eye.

"I've been riding long enough to get comfortable back in the saddle quickly when the occasion arises," William replied.

"I would lay a bet that you can't outride me any more. Remember when we used to jump together? Even then, I was always the better rider," Yannick said, with a mock solemn expression on his handsome face.

"I know where this is going, Yannick." William raised an eyebrow. He turned to Grace. "Any moment now, Yannick will propose that we set up a show-jumping course in the sand school."

"Well, I wasn't going to, but now you mention it…" Yannick grinned.

William rolled his eyes but smiled back. "Fine, nine one-metre fences, the rider with the least faults wins. Stephen will adjudicate."

Yannick spread his hands. "An excellent proposal! Let us go and see our horses for today."

They walked towards the barn, where the heads of ten magnificent horses showed at the half doors of their stalls.

It was going to be a fine day of fun with his old friend, William thought.

Chapter 14 – Dog Does Not Eat Dog

Brescia, Italy, 2000

Francesco looked out of the window. The city had changed so much over the years he'd known it. It had grown, but in growing, it had become darker, more dangerous, more anonymous. The sense of connection and warmth had gone. It wasn't familiar to him any more. The shoeshine boys were long gone. He glanced at his own well-polished handmade shoes – he rarely saw anyone wearing properly cared-for shoes any more. And where were the market traders who had known each customer by name? He sighed. Maybe the city didn't recognise him any more, either.

He returned his attention to the matter at hand. The boardroom table felt too large for two people to sit at comfortably, which is why he'd chosen to conduct the meeting here rather than in his office.

He examined the bottles in the drinks cabinet, selected a bottle of Amaro and poured two measures into crystal tumblers.

Carlo continued to gaze at him in astonishment.

"I thought it would be a consolation to you to know that after the unexpected death of your father-in-law, the company would be in good hands," he said, pushing a glass over to Carlo.

"I expected those hands to be my hands."

"And you will still play an important part in the company. Under my direction."

Carlo was beginning to turn red. "I have always been good to you, Franco."

"And I am repaying that kindness by giving you a role in the company."

"I had plans for the company, for expansion."

"And I have bigger plans. I am expanding my import/export metals business. The connections your father-in-law made for this company with some prominent figures in, shall we say, non-governmental waste disposal, will play a key role in my future business."

Carlo banged his fist on the desk, sending ripples through their glasses of Amaro. "All these years, you've always refused when I asked if you wanted in on these deals."

Francesco watched the ripples die away.

"Yes. Because then you were proposing that I do business with you, Carlo. Now, I'm proposing that you do business with me." He picked up his drink and swirled it gently. "Of course, you have the right to decline."

Carlo gave a hollow laugh. "I understand the sort of choice you are offering me. It is no choice at all."

"There is always a choice. My businesses are expanding rapidly. If we find we can work well together, you will have many opportunities."

"And if we don't work well together?"

"Then, sadly, there will not be."

Carlo was silent. "Then welcome to the family," he said at last.

Chapter 15 – Isaiah 60:17

Ashanti Region, Ghana, January 2021

The regional minister rose from the ornate mahogany table when Francesco was shown into the hotel conference room.

"It is an honour to meet you, Minister Amoah-Mensah," Francesco said respectfully, offering his hand.

"John, please," said the minister affably.

They took their seats. Fans whirred overhead, chilling the sweat on the back of Francesco's neck.

He was used to the heat of Italy in the summertime, but the heat in Kumasi was intense and unrelenting and left him feeling drunk with tiredness by the evening.

It had been bearable at the mining sites, out in the river-threaded, heavily forested countryside. In the city, the blazing sun bounced off the buildings and baked man, woman, child and dog alike to death.

"How have you enjoyed your trip so far?" the minister asked.

"It has been a privilege to see the beauty and abundance of the land and to be treated with such hospitality by her people," Francesco said.

"I am pleased that you have had the opportunity to visit the countryside. As you will have seen, we have so many under-utilised resources due to the bureaucratic limitations placed upon us," the minister replied.

"I believe I can offer you some significant opportunities for regional development," Francesco said as the minister poured them glasses of a chilled ginger and lemon drink that seemed to help keep heatstroke at bay – Lamugin, he'd heard it called.

The ice clinked lazily against the sides of the jug, and Francesco relished the coolness of the sound.

"So my colleagues have told me," the minister said, his voice mild and smooth.

Francesco looked at him. He was neatly attired in an airy linen suit with expensive Italian shoes – handmade, he thought.

The minister's manner was gentle and friendly, but Francesco had spent time building a picture of this man and knew this was a superficial veneer. The illegal mines were built on human suffering. There was blood on the hands of each and every person involved with them. The man was dangerous, brutal and deeply corrupt.

Which suited his needs perfectly.

"As you are aware," Francesco said, running his forefinger through the cool condensation on his glass, "I have extensive expertise, resources and operations in the metal industry. I have spent the last thirty years building my business. My international shipping and freight network is well-established, my smelting and refining operations in Italy are efficient, skilled and well-staffed, and my connections with…" he paused to add emphasis to his words "…buyers looking for discreet access to gold and related items are unparalleled."

This, Francesco thought, was the reward for the countless years of lunches and dinners with representatives from crime families and organisations from Sicily to Majorca to Kosovo and beyond.

"I am aware of your impressive reputation," the minister said, with a bow of his head.

"I believe that the current small-scale artisanal nature of the mining operations I viewed in the region are capable of significant mechanisation and improvements," Francesco added.

118

The minister spread his hands. "Indeed they are, but there are three problems for us. Firstly, we lack the funds for expansion. Secondly, we lack the means to get the gold out of the country now that the Dubai route has been suppressed. Thirdly, if we solve the first two problems, we are left with the challenge of how to process the increased proceeds to a satisfactory extent, although I believe I could resolve this issue."

"I can resolve the first two issues," Francesco said, leaning his chin casually on his hand but holding the minister's gaze. "I will offer investment for expansion of your mines, and I will establish an alternate route to move the gold. What is your suggestion for the resolution of the third?"

"Ah, that is simple. You buy diamonds of good provenance for me in Europe, and I take these as payment and resell them," the minister said with a smile.

"An admirably simple solution," Francesco agreed.

***

Brescia, Italy, April 2021

Francesco sat listening to the endless droning of the priest. The stone church and hard pews made for a cheerless setting, despite the grand frescos touched with gilt and bright colours and the ornate pillars framing the aisle. A statue of Santa Lucia gazed impassively down at him from her niche, the dish containing her eyes held casually in her hand. Francesco had always found the figure gruesome.

His mother was sitting next to him, her rosary in her hand. At almost eighty years old, she looked small and birdlike. The heaviness of loss had bowed her shoulders a little, but she was still sharp and vigorous.

He came for her alone. She, he knew, took comfort in the thought that Laura and Rosa lay in the arms of the

Lord. He, however, could take no comfort in the idea of a God who could be cruel enough to take them from him.

The priest was giving his homily. Francesco gritted his teeth. He found the smugness of the priest's pious expression intensely irritating. He gazed at him, wondering what it would be like to punch the man's bulbous nose, to feel it squash under his knuckles and witness the wounded astonishment as the priest dabbed at the blood streaming from his nose. His mother coughed, rousing him from his reverie. Francesco tried to concentrate on the priest's words.

"The Lord transforms all," the priest was saying. "Hate to love, grief to joy, the bare earth to the harvest."

Francesco dropped his eyes to the stone-flagged floor to stop himself from rolling them to the heavens with irritation. The Lord had done nothing for his grief.

"The Lord tells us this, with great grace, in Isaiah 60:17"

> Instead of bronze, I will bring you gold
> and silver in place of iron.
> Instead of wood, I will bring you bronze,
> and iron in place of stones.
> I will make peace your governor
> and wellbeing your ruler.

Francesco blinked. Instead of bronze, I will bring you gold. He ran the phrase over and over in his head and laughed aloud.

His mother stared at him in horror and nudged him hard with her elbow.

He smothered his laughter and bowed his head in apology, trying to transform the laugh into a cough. Hushed voices rippled in the pews around them as people turned their heads discreetly in search of the source of the disruption.

His mother frowned at him a little but returned her attention to the priest. Francesco made a show of pulling a handkerchief from his pocket to dab his face, feigning indisposition.

Bronze into gold. That was the key.

Francesco sat back in the pew, smiling. This was developing well. He would turn the small-scale artisan mines in Ashanti into high-yielding mines with his investment and expertise, and they would be reliant on him for supporting and maintaining production as well as selling the gold and washing the proceeds.

Now he had the final piece in the puzzle of how to move large volumes of gold without attracting notice.

He pressed his hands together in a gesture of prayer with genuine gratitude for the first time in many years.

Thank you, Lord.

Chapter 16 – The Freeport

Grace looked along the row of half doors at the horses. Each one was beautiful – their coats glistening with health and care.

Yannick spoke to a stable hand, giving instructions to set up single, double and wide oxers, with the front and back fences set to different heights in the sand school, before returning to them.

"Grace, you will be riding this gentle girl today. Her name is Epona. After William and I have had our little competition, the stable hand will find you a suitable saddle and help you groom her so that you can get to know her," Yannick said.

Grace looked at the beautiful black mare with deep, gentle brown eyes. Grace held her hand out. The horse pushed her nose towards her curiously and allowed Grace to gently stroke her silky neck.

"Stephen – Apollo is for you." Yannick gestured to an enormous light chestnut horse. "I assume that you and William brought your saddles with you."

Stephen nodded. "They're in the car. I'll go and get them."

"And for you, William, we have Loki." A dark bay horse snorted in a stall, looking haughtily down at them from his imposing height.

"Loki?" William said with a quizzical look.

"He suits his name," Yannick said with a smile.

"Will you be riding Chantilly?" William asked.

"Yes," Yannick said, his smile warming as he walked over to a golden mare with a pale cream mane.

Chantilly reminded Grace of a toy horse she had as a child. She was an impossibly pretty horse with delicate lines and an almost iridescent sheen to her coat.

Stephen returned with the saddles, and he and Grace took a seat in the shade, chatting while they watched Yannick and William brush their horses before saddling up. Chantilly stood obediently for Yannick as he brushed her down and patiently allowed him to put on her bridle. Loki, however, snorted and tossed his head as William worked with him, speaking softly to him as he stroked him and worked with him to ready him for their ride. Stephen was grinning.

"I have a feeling that Yannick has stacked the odds against William," Grace said.

"Well, that's a stunning horse he's given him, but he is as spirited as his name suggests," Stephen said, watching as William led out Loki, who stepped briskly out of his stall, pulling at his bridle.

They followed Yannick and William down to the sand school. Grace joined Stephen, leaning on the guardrail, the rough wood warm from the sun under her hands.

William and Yannick walked their horses around the school, allowing them to loosen up, before moving the horses up through their paces, trotting and cantering around the arena.

As William came towards the part of the arena where they stood, Grace felt the heavy, rhythmic thud of Loki's hooves on the ground, dust and the smell of sand rising as they thundered past. Loki had his head down, frisking and snorting as he fought William for control of his head, for a while, until William's smooth control brought him in line, moving pistonlike over the ground.

Yannick and Chantilly moved together like dancers, the rise and fall of the horse and rider perfectly aligned.

Grace turned to Stephen and raised an eyebrow. "Do you think William has a chance of winning?"

Stephen shrugged. "They are both excellent riders and excellent show-jumpers. Yannick has the home advantage, but William is doing well in working with Loki."

"And this is all part of the delicate art of diplomacy, I guess," Grace added.

Stephen inclined his head. "Yannick wants to get the most out of his day with William since he's doing him a favour. They may as well have a little sport while we're here."

Yannick and William had slowed the horses down to a walk. William raised his hand to Stephen, who gave a thumbs-up in return.

"They're ready. I'll be keeping score," Stephen explained to Grace. "I'll be watching for faults – where the horse makes contact with and brings down the poles."

Yannick and William rode over to join them at the railings.

"William, I was thinking that to make this a little more fun, we should agree a prize for the winner. What do you think?"

"What did you have in mind?"

Yannick glanced down at Grace and winked. "The winner takes Grace for dinner."

William stiffened. "Absolutely not, Yannick. What are we, medieval knights jousting for a woman's favour?"

Stephen nudged Grace's ribs and she stifled a giggle. "Oh, I don't mind, William, I rather like the idea."

He gritted his teeth. "It's plain old-fashioned misogyny."

"Come, don't take it so seriously!" Yannick laughed.

Grace smiled innocently. "I agree. Go ahead, I get a good dinner with a charming man whoever wins."

"Fine," William growled, touching Loki with his heels and moving away.

Yannick followed, grinning at his retreating back.

"Well, this will be interesting," Stephen said, with a laugh.

Yannick rode first. Grace watched him navigate the course, Chantilly sailing elegantly over the jumps, Yannick moving gracefully with her. She took the single, double and oxers effortlessly.

"No faults," Stephen called out.

William moved to the start of the course. Loki tossed his head and pranced sideways for a moment before William tapped him into motion, urging him forward over the first jump. Loki cleared the single jump well but still capered and frisked under William's control.

"If he wants that dinner, he'll need to put a little more leg on over the oxers and keep the horse straight," Stephen said.

William regained control, and they rounded the corner. Loki moved forward into the deep oxer, clearing the first and second jumps cleanly, hooves thudding into the sand as he landed, sending dust billowing into the air.

They cleared the rest of the jumps. Their style was markedly different to that of Yannick and Chantilly. Where Yannick and Chantilly were refined and streamlined in their movements, William and Loki were raw power, each jump a battle of wills to contain and channel the horse's pure, wild energy.

"No faults," Stephen called out again.

"What happens now?" Grace asked.

"A second round," Stephen said, "but with higher fences. The stable hand will set them to one metre twenty." The stable hand was briskly working his way around the arena, resetting each fence. Once he'd finished, Stephen raised his hand to indicate that they could start.

Yannick started his second run. Chantilly moved over the jumps like warm butter, her lines beautifully clean.

"No faults," Stephen said as they completed the course.

William took Loki to the start of the circuit. The horse snorted and pulled, eager to dive into the jumps, kicking his hindquarters into the air as they set off, before settling under William's hands and heels. This time, Loki worked more smoothly with William, and they surged over the jumps, leaving the air full of the rumble of hooves and the clean, fresh smell of horse sweat.

"No faults, time-trial tiebreaker, first six fences!" Stephen called. He turned to Grace. "Do you have a stopwatch?"

Grace pulled up the stopwatch on her phone.

"Good, this time, you track their time. I'll be looking out for faults."

The stable hand, who had been watching from across the arena, hopped in and moved some of the fences out of the way to create a shorter course.

"Quickest to complete six fences wins," Stephen called out.

Grace readied the stopwatch. Yannick positioned himself at the start. Chantilly pranced a little in a delicate show of impatience, shaking her mane in the breeze. Yannick patted her neck.

Grace raised a hand to show she had the stopwatch ready. Yannick moved off. Chantilly was swift as the wind, they cleared the first five fences with grace and style, but as she approached the sixth, Stephen breathed in, as Chantilly came steaming towards the fence too low. She clipped the top pole with her rear hooves as she cleared the fence, setting it rattling, but it stayed put. Stephen breathed out softly. Grace stopped the watch – 38.6 seconds.

Yannick slowed Chantilly to a walk as William and Loki approached the start of the course.

Loki shook his head and snorted, head low as he waited for William to let him move off. Grace gave a thumbs-up to show she had the watch ready. Loki moved into the first fence with great speed. He almost didn't pull up enough to clear the poles, belly nearly skimming the pole as he cleared it and continued on, dancing sideways until William brought him back under control as they approached the next fence. They cleared fence after fence, powering through the course, sweat shining on horse and man, until they swept over the last fence, Loki's muscles bunching and releasing in a smooth, powerful burst. Grace stopped the watch – 37.8.

Stephen glanced at the stopwatch. "Do you want to announce it?" he said, grinning.

"Yannick – 38.6 seconds, William – 37.8 seconds. We have our winner. Congratulations to my dinner companion. I'll be expecting lobster," Grace called, laughing as Yannick and William dismounted and shook hands, clapping each other on the back.

"Well, that's the duties of diplomacy fulfilled," she said softly to Stephen, "although I think it would have been more gentlemanly of William to let Yannick win."

Stephen chuckled. "No, it had to be a fair game – it shows true respect for your fellow competitor to give your full effort, and besides, did you really think he'd let Yannick take you for dinner?"

***

"Why do freeports exist?" Grace asked Yannick as they rode side by side along a wide, pretty path through the forest at the edge of his land.

"They are designed to increase economic activity," Yannick said. "Goods coming into freeports are exempt from taxes, and that helps to encourage increased trading."

"But doesn't that automatically increase the risk of criminals taking advantage of this to help launder the proceeds of crime?" Grace said.

"Yes, it does," Yannick replied with a grin, "but they are very profitable, so most governments agree that the benefits outweigh the costs."

Grace nodded. She thought about her own work in the prisons. Corruption rings were all pretty much the same, regardless of size. The key ingredients of systemic weaknesses – individuals motivated to make a profit, or who had been compromised and left vulnerable to blackmail, and a lack of action at a strategic level to prevent corruption – were present whether you were talking about a covert black-market shop on a prison wing or an international smuggling operation. This was on a larger scale, with different players, but it was the same game.

Stephen and William were riding ahead of them. They made imposing figures on their horses – Grace imagined they must have looked magnificent in their dress uniforms for the Household Cavalry.

They rode easily, chatting as they went down the path, waiting to come into a clearing Yannick wanted to take them to for a picnic lunch.

The trees thinned and opened out to a clearing, bathed in dappled sunlight, with benches and a table in a wooden pavilion at the centre. They left the horses grazing happily on the sweet young grass next to the pavilion while Yannick unpacked their lunch.

A selection of fragrant rosti, still warm, beautiful bread, local butter, cheeses, cured meats, salads and a hearty sliced sausage flavoured with cumin filled the table. Yannick produced a bottle of good white wine, glasses, plates and cutlery and urged them to eat.

As they talked, Grace sat back and observed Yannick and William running through the social rituals of enquiries about family and mutual friends and updates on horses and dogs.

"And what brings you to Geneva this time, apart from the pleasure of my company?" Yannick asked.

"Ah, an intrigue, Yannick. One I am hoping you can help us with," William replied, patting his friend's arm companionably.

"Involving the Freeport, you mentioned on the telephone," Yannick said.

"Yes, we think that the Freeport may be the fulcrum for a gold-smuggling operation," William said.

"It is very challenging to get information regarding trade within the Freeport," Yannick said seriously. "The information is maintained under conditions of the highest security."

"I know I am asking a lot, Yannick," William conceded.

"There'll be a price," Yannick said.

William raised an eyebrow.

"I want a puppy from one of your girls when you breed them," he said with a grin.

William laughed. "Yannick, you know that was always on the cards."

"It doesn't hurt to add the weight of obligation to an agreement," Yannick said.

"So that means you'll try to help us?" William smiled.

"Of course. What do you need?" asked Yannick.

"We suspect that the money from the gold smuggling is being laundered through diamond trades and that these might be coming through the Freeport. We have a list of companies that we believe may be involved. If you can get us a list of accounts with significantly increased trades over the last year and links to Tunisia and Italy, that may help to give us a strong lead," William said.

"No problem. Give me forty-eight hours, and I'll get you the information."

***

Amira's face looked out at them from a light-filled studio in Milan. Gerrard, somewhere in his vast mansion in San Francisco, had his camera and mic turned off while he went to speak to a member of his staff.

"Yannick's list has enabled Gerrard and me to narrow down our initial shortlist further. There are two companies, one based in Tunisia, and one based in Italy, who have shown increased activity in the Freeport accounts listings – I think it is worth running active surveillance on both. I have been tracking their charters – both are running large amounts of cargo to and from Africa," Amira said.

Gerrard returned to the screen. "We've acquired the bills of lading for the Tunisian and Italian companies."

Their inboxes pinged as a document reached them.

Grace scanned through them. They detailed the items the vessel was transporting, their weight and their value. The Tunisian company seemed to be trading in scrap metals. The Italian company also traded in scrap metals on the outward voyages and, on the return voyages, shipped refined metals. Bronze, steel, zinc, brass.

"What do we know about these two companies?" she asked.

"The Italian company – Castelli – is owned by an established entrepreneur, Francesco Castelli. It has seen massive growth over the last few decades. Our intelligence indicates some links with underworld figures. The Tunisian company – Euro-metál, is a large-scale operation with interests primarily in recycling. They, too, have links to governmental corruption and organised crime. It is run by a shady conglomerate of businessmen," Gerrard said.

"They both seem promising suspects," Grace said.

"Wait…" Amira said, pulling up one of the pages onto their screen. "This shipment by Castelli – the bill of lading reports a cargo of bronze and brass ingots, but the weights are off. It's heavier than it should be," she said.

Gerrard's fingers flew over his keyboard. "OK, look at this," he said, sending a screenshot of an inspection sheet onto the screen. "That shipment was inspected by port authorities in Tunisia – it matched the bill of lading, and no issues were detected."

"So, either Castelli is bribing officials, or the gold was concealed in the cargo," Grace said.

William nodded. "Amira, when is the next Castelli shipment due through Tunisia? Do you have their charters?" he asked.

"Let me check." Amira paused, searching through the documents in her project folder. "Their next vessel is due to come into the port of La Goulette in Tunis in three days," she replied. "Euro-metál have a shipment due soon, but the details aren't available yet. Once we receive that info, we'll have an idea whether they might also be a contender."

Grace tapped her fingers on the table thoughtfully. "Could both companies be involved?"

Amira shrugged. "Possibly. Until we get the information about their shipment, it's hard to tell. My money would be on Euro-metál, of the two companies. Tunisia's location makes shipping from a number of African regions known to have issues with illegal gold mining easier."

"Well, it's a waiting game until we get that information," William said.

"Cartier are throwing a party in Barcelona to launch their new high-end jewellery collection, if you want to come," Amira said. "I modelled for the launch campaign, so I have to go, but your company would make it much more enjoyable."

"The Diamond is not far from Barcelona, and it gives us a chance to update in person as new information comes in," William said thoughtfully. "Let's do that. Gerrard – can you join us?"

"I'll see you there."

Amira and Gerrard signed off, leaving the screen blank.

"Does the party count as your winning dinner date with me?" Grace asked with a smile.

"Oh, no." William gave a wolfish grin. "I'll take my prize at a time of my choosing. I haven't forgotten."

Chapter 17 – Barcelona

William gestured for Grace to take his arm as the waiting attendant nodded respectfully and unclipped the rope. The grand double flights of steps to Park Güell rose up in front of them, clothed in red carpet. They walked up the stairs arm in arm. William enjoyed the soft pressure of her body against him.

Grace was dressed in an immaculately cut green silk dress that perfectly set off her dark hair and pale skin. The evening was still warm, and the golden light of the hour before sunset lit the pale stone of the fantastical structures of the park beautifully.

"Have you been here before?" he asked.

She shook her head.

"Gaudi built this place as a housing estate for Barcelona's elite – it was designed as a great garden city, inspired by English designs of the time, but it became a public park and pleasure ground instead."

They reached the top of the stairs, arriving in an open-sided hall filled with lofty Grecian columns beneath an ornately tiled ceiling.

"This is beautiful," Grace said.

The hall was beginning to fill up. A string quartet played, their music drifting out over the gardens and partygoers mingled in knots. William spotted Amira and waved. She made her way over to them. She was dressed in a simple black dress that allowed the sumptuously hued Cartier jewels to shine. A waiter arrived, bringing glasses of champagne. Amira took one and handed another to Grace, kissing her and William and exclaiming over Grace's dress.

"It's good to see you both. Have you seen Gerrard?"

William shook his head. "He was chasing some final pieces of information and said he would be a little late to the party."

"Then let's meet in the square when he gets here. Duty calls."

She moved off to speak to a photographer, who had been hovering, eager to take advantage of the light.

William turned to Grace. "Care to explore the gardens with me?"

They wandered along the palm-tree-lined paths, admiring the views out over Barcelona. The city stretched out before them in the clear evening light, the sea a glittering blue line beyond the tangle of buildings.

"Do you enjoy these parties?" Grace asked.

"Sometimes. I like the surroundings – and the company – tonight. Celebrities and models can be a bore, but as Amira said, attendance is often a matter of duty. Social events like these are often the grease on the wheels of big business. From a Moonlight Society perspective, maintaining and growing our contacts through having a presence at this sort of function is essential."

William gestured around them to the small groups of people talking. "Look around. That man there–" he indicated with his champagne glass to a stocky older man "–he's a duke. He has significant land ownership across the most expensive areas of London. The blonde woman he's talking to owns one of Europe's largest commercial development companies. Their talk is likely to be about more than the jewellery launch and the quality of the canapés."

They walked on, finding a seat on a bench overlooking the gardens.

"That woman there–" Grace followed his gaze "–she's the daughter of a Sicilian Mafia don. She's talking to the owners of a prominent shipping company and a pharmaceutical company. I'll leave their potential common interests to your imagination."

"I see," Grace said. "How about those two over there?" She nodded towards two men standing beneath the trees, deep in conversation.

"Oh, that is the owner of the company that owns most of the fibre infrastructure in Europe. He's someone we like to keep an eye on. There is a spot off the coast of Ireland where the undersea cabling connects the United Kingdom and Ireland to the rest of Europe and the United States. It's particularly vulnerable to attack, so maintaining security and continually upgrading the protection and surveillance of the area is vital to protecting telecommunications and information security."

"And who is the other man?" Grace leaned forward, a look of curiosity on her face.

"A Russian oligarch."

Grace raised her eyebrows. "Oh, that doesn't seem good."

William smiled. "Don't worry, both of them are on our side. Besides, they are probably talking about racing."

"Horses?"

"No, Grand Touring cars, GT3."

Grace sat back and scanned the people around her. "Any politicians?"

William smiled. "Of course. See the man in the silver tuxedo? He's a New York mayoral candidate and former presidential advisor."

Grace narrowed her eyes. "I think I recognise him, now you mention it. Wasn't he involved in some Mafia money laundering scandal?"

"Yes, that's right. You'll probably notice him avoiding being seen with the don's daughter, but they know each other very well."

"How well?"

"Very well."

"Oh." Grace was quiet for a moment. "I see why it's important for Moonlight Society members to attend these parties. It must be an intelligence-gathering dream."

"Yes, and these are difficult circles for traditional intelligence agencies to infiltrate because they are so closed."

Grace laughed. "Lucky I'm your plus one, I guess. I'd never get a seat at the table otherwise."

William frowned. "You're here because you are talented, knowledgeable and brilliant. Never forget that."

Grace blushed, absent-mindedly running her fingers over her necklace. She lifted her empty glass. "Shall we pick up a refill on our way to find Gerrard and Amira?"

They walked over to a bar set up in the square. The sun had begun to set, and lights twinkled on tables along the long balcony overlooking the city.

"More champagne or a cocktail?" William asked.

"How about a champagne cocktail?"

William signalled for the bartender. "Two French 75s, please – with Krug Grand Cuvée, if you have it."

"Yes, sir." The bartender moved around the bar efficiently, preparing their drinks.

Grace looked at William curiously. "A French 75?"

"Gin, champagne, lemon and sugar – named after a 75 mm artillery field gun."

"Ah. With the combination of gin and champagne, I can understand why."

The bartender slid their drinks over to them.

"Sláinte."

"Cheers."

Amira and Gerrard joined them.

They found a table at a distance from the others.

"Updates?" William asked.

Gerrard inclined his head. "Several. The bills of lading for Euro-métal look clean and consistent. It seems unlikely they are involved, but when digging for intelligence on Euro-métal, I came across something interesting."

Amira leaned in. "Connections between the companies?"

"Right. Francesco Castelli has been pushing to buy out Euro-métal," Gerrard continued.

"Why Euro-métal?" Grace asked, eyeing Gerrard with interest.

"Euro-métal probably caught Castelli's attention for the same reason they caught ours – the companies have several shared areas of business. However, Castelli's connections are primarily with Ghana. Euro-métal has a more extensive network of contacts and trade routes across South and Central Africa."

Amira shook her head. "Regions with existing issues with illegal mining, who have previously had to rely on sending their gold out to Asian and Middle Eastern markets, including Dubai. He is looking to expand his smuggling operations significantly. At this rate, he's got to be on track to become a serious global contender, bringing illegal gold into Europe in a way that hasn't previously been possible."

Gerrard sighed heavily. "There's more. I managed to track Castelli's movements over the last six months. He's visited some rural sites in the Ashanti region in Ghana. The number of deaths suspected to be related to illegal mining activity in the area has increased significantly. Aerial footage indicates the Ashanti mines have expanded rapidly. I think he's driving production, as well as arranging distribution."

Grace gave a low whistle. "A formidable man – sounds like he's aiming for vertical integration up and down the production process. It's something you see with really sophisticated organised crime."

William drummed his fingers on the table. "We need to stamp this out now. The more his operations grow, the harder it will be to take him down. Stephen, Grace and I will head to Tunis. We'll try to gather sufficient evidence to support Interpol to move on Castelli. Gerrard, I'll need you covering our backs with surveillance, comms and intelligence. Amira, we'll need your knowledge of metals to help us make sense of what we are seeing once we get eyes on the ground."

He turned to Grace. "We should return to the Diamond, brief Stephen and ready ourselves for the flight to Tunisia."

Chapter 18 – Barcelona to Tunis

William stared out of the car window – they'd picked up an R32 Golf. Fast and not too eye-catching, it handled the intense, rambunctious traffic well, nipping through the city.

Their villa was on the outskirts of the town. The main road outside was grey and industrial, but the villa had been planted all around with lush gardens that deadened the noise of the traffic and created a sense of serenity.

The house was a modern, square, white building, airy and cool. William walked into the main living space. It looked out onto a private garden with a pool. He scanned his surroundings. It was pleasant – stone floors and large windows, complemented by neutral linen and light woods. Antique rugs and ceramics added touches of richness. William made a quick security check. The large windows and walls backed onto other houses. The side entrance of the house, with a gate to the road, was more vulnerable than he liked. He glanced across at Stephen, who was looking out of the window. He turned and met William's eye and gave a slight shrug.

Grace had gone to unpack in her bedroom. William had directed her to the room between his and Stephen's. If someone entered from the rear or through the front door, her bedroom wouldn't be the first one they'd reach.

Lunch was laid out for them on the long dining table.

William sat down and looked at Grace and Stephen. "We know that the shipment coming in tomorrow morning is highly likely to be carrying smuggled gold.

Grace, what are your thoughts on our strategy from a psychological perspective?"

"In large-scale operations like this, it's quite possible that the majority of the crew will have no knowledge of any issues with the cargo – the accurate reporting of its weight which created the discrepancy that raised our suspicions highlights this." She tapped her fingers on the table.

"They are clearly unaware that there is anything to hide. These crew members are likely to be fairly calm and are unlikely to be aggressive and hostile on approach."

She glanced up at them. "However, in most cases, one or two key players will be present who are aware of the true nature of the operation. These are the people who are most likely to pose a risk to us. If they feel that we know anything that might endanger the operation, they may seek to stop us from sharing that information through the use of violence or through kidnap and interrogation to try to make sense of how much we know and how widely that information is known," she said.

"I think security and discretion are key here," Stephen added.

William nodded. "The shipment will be sitting in a warehouse near the port tonight, ready for loading tomorrow morning. I suggest we go in tonight, after dark, and get some footage of the cargo. We have body-worn cameras, and Gerrard and his team will be offering remote surveillance and support. His team will be able to act if we get into difficulties and are unable to call for help. As long as we can get a look at the cargo, we'll have some information to push forward with, enabling Interpol to make their move. Currently, they have insufficient data to justify a raid on Castelli."

"I'll take the handheld digital scales," Stephen said. "We'll get some additional data on weights for Amira, if we can."

"Good plan." William turned and looked at Grace. "If there is any emerging threat of aggression, our first objective is to get out, as rapidly as we can, back to the car and back here. If Stephen and I have to hold off attackers, your objective is to get out of sight and somewhere safe. Do you understand?"

Grace rolled her eyes. "I understand. I don't like it, but I understand. If I try to help, I'm more likely to get taken hostage, and that would distract you and Stephen from dealing with the main threat."

"Right. I mean, you've done well in training, but Stephen and I have had a lot longer to train," William said, trying to reassure Grace that this wasn't an issue of capability but of practicality.

"I know," she replied. "Same as in the prison – as a civilian, your first job is to get out of the way of the officers so they can deal with the situation without having to worry about you as well as everything else going down."

"Right. Exactly that," Stephen agreed. "Although I wouldn't want to be on the receiving end of one of your punches." He grinned.

"Gerrard has had his drones out to spot our exits and escape routes, should we need them," William said. "His intelligence gathering suggests that there are only two security guards on site after 8 p.m. We make our move at midnight."

***

Grace peeped out of the car, hunched down in the back seat as they pulled into La Goulette. It was an ugly port, grimy, industrial and functional. Floodlights spaced along the perimeter fence made pools of brightness, surrounded by deep shadows.

Stephen cut the car's lights and edged the car into a dark spot near the warehouse.

140

They inched towards the entrance. Each of them was kitted out with earpieces, a body-worn camera strapped to their chest and night-vision goggles.

"The security guards are playing cards by the front entrance." Gerrard's voice came over their earpieces. "Follow the warehouse wall to your left and go in via the back door. It's secured with a Yale lock. There's no active door alarm."

Stephen kept watch as William pulled out a set of picks. He selected one and inserted it into the lock, wiggling it until the levers clicked. He pushed the door open and gestured them inside.

A long walkway ran down the length of the warehouse.

"Head for area B," Gerrard said.

Grace followed William as they stalked down through the dark. Stephen was close behind her.

Area D. Area C. Area B. They spread out along the aisle, ensuring their cameras scanned each pallet as they passed. William raised a hand to catch their attention and pointed. In front of him, a row of pallets of metal ingots was tightly taped with strapping marked 'Castelli'. Stephen took out a knife and eased it under the taut tape, stretching it outwards.

"Grace," he hissed, "can you get your fingers under here and pull an ingot out?"

She moved to his side. The bars of metal were closely packed, but she managed to get a grip on one of them, inching it out. Stephen put out his large hands, the digital scale resting on his palms. Grace rested the bar on the scale. The red display lights flashed as it calculated the weight.

"Are you receiving data from the scale, Gerrard?" he asked.

"Received."

Stephen nodded at Grace. She took the ingot and began sliding it carefully back into place.

William frowned and held up a hand. They froze.

"Any movement from the guards?" he whispered.

There was silence from their earpieces. Grace stared at William. He was frowning.

"I think we've lost comms," Stephen breathed. ·

"We need to get out." William pushed the ingot back in place with the heel of his hand and thrust Grace behind him.

"Incoming, incoming!" Gerrard's voice crackled over the airwaves, before there was again silence.

William took Grace's hand and ran back down the walkway, Stephen hard on their heels.

They reached the door and William threw it open. Outside, two flashlights pointed at them.

Grace skidded to a halt, almost slamming into William's back.

"Run!" William barked. He thrust one of the guards aside, sending him to the ground. Grace sprinted past him, and the second man gave chase, almost catching up with her.

Stephen walloped the back of the guard's head as he passed, sending him flying.

William hauled open the car door. Grace tried to get in, but the guards were upon them. A truck slewed across their path and another two men ran over, joining the guards.

William and Stephen moved to put her between them. A plank from a broken pallet lay in the dust at her feet. Grace scooped it up and held it in front of her, trying to keep all of the men in her eye-line at once.

The men surged forward and tried to force Stephen and William back. Grace moved between them, trying not to get under their feet as they fought back. William kicked out at a man who ducked under his reach to get behind them. Grace threw the piece of wood into his hands, and William spun it in a scything motion, forcing the men back.

One of the men pushed forward, sweeping between Stephen and William with a kick that landed hard in Grace's ribs. She crumpled with the impact. Stephen caught her arms and pulled her back to her feet as William punched the blunt end of the wood into the man's face, sending blood splattering from his nose.

William looked down at Grace, frowning. She gave him a brief smile, breathing hard. He nodded and turned back to the men.

Stephen used his immense reach to force another man back with a flurry of kicks, but a third dodged behind them, blocking the car doors.

William hit out at him with the plank of wood, sending him pitching forward into the dust. Stephen pushed him away and opened the door, shoving Grace into the back seat.

He jumped in, William close behind and they roared out onto the port road.

"Gerrard?" William was breathing hard.

"Here. Two of Castelli's men showed up in a white truck. They're on your tail."

"Got it." Stephen slammed the brakes on to slew the car sideways onto a piece of waste ground. He cut the lights and the truck carried on past them. He pulled back out and doubled back to take the opposite exit out of the port. They drove on in silence, each of them focused on the road.

"I can't see anyone following us," Grace said.

"You're clear." Gerrard said, relief in his voice. "And we got enough data from the visuals and scales to produce a 3-D image of the ingot. Amira's working on analysis now."

"Great." William nodded his approval. "Let's convene a meeting tomorrow morning."

They pulled into the drive of their villa. Stephen drew the car out of sight behind the gates.

"That was close. I didn't think we were going to get out of there." Grace let out a long sigh as they bolted the door behind them.

William grinned. "We've been through worse." He took Grace's hand and led her through to her room.

She was shaking, adrenaline coursing through her veins.

He rubbed her arms, bringing warmth to her chilled skin. "You did well, there," he said, his voice soft. "Are you hurt?"

Grace shook her head.

William narrowed his eyes. "Show me the ribs."

Grace pulled up her T-shirt, wincing slightly. It was torn, and there was a little blood on it. She wasn't sure if it was her own or from the guy William had hit in the face.

She looked down. Her ribs were already starting to turn black and purple, and there was a scrape where the edge of the man's boot had grazed her skin, which was sticky and bloody.

"OK, let's get this cleaned," William said. "We really should get a medic, but this one is within my range of skills." He grinned.

Grace laughed, then grimaced as the movement sent a spasm of pain through her.

"Do you think they're broken?" she said.

William slid his fingers over her side, gently probing. "Take a deep breath, if you can."

She took a breath. It hurt. A lot. But she could draw breath.

"No, I don't think so, but we'll get them checked out if you have any problems breathing." William gently put his palm against her ribs, as if feeling how they moved as she breathed. His hand was warm, large on her small frame. Grace looked down at his strong, powerful hand. He could almost encircle her ribcage with his big hands.

He eased his hand to the other side of her chest, fingers gently probing for damage.

Grace's heart quickened at his touch, despite the pain that stabbed at her each time she drew breath.

She was still looking down at his hand when his fingers stopped their journey and she lifted her eyes. He was looking at her keenly, his eyes filled with concern. She fought to push down the flickers of desire that she felt sure were written across her face, but as Grace looked into his eyes, she saw the echo of her own want and need.

She dropped her eyes. William left his hand on her ribs for a long moment, and she relished the heat of his skin.

"I'll clean this graze for you," he said, walking from the room. He returned with a first-aid kit and proceeded to clean the raw, sticky abrasion.

Grace tried to ignore the feeling of his sure, gentle fingers as he worked to meticulously clean the graze. Finally, satisfied with his work, William covered the wound neatly with a dressing.

"Well, we should pack up, then eat before we hit the road. Once the adrenaline wears off, we'll all be tired, hungry and irritable," he said, grinning at her.

"Good plan," Grace replied automatically. "Where are we going?"

"Back to the Diamond. She was sailing towards Italy due to the intelligence Amira provided us with. We'll pick her up in Palermo and reconvene the team there."

Chapter 19 – Lost and Found

Brescia, Italy, 2022

Francesco sat in his office. It looked out across the same factory his father had worked in. No matter how large his business had become, he still liked to come here, to sit at the small, plain desk and listen to the sounds of the men as they worked.

He mapped out in his head the distribution for the incoming delivery – Kosovo, Majorca, Sicily and Ireland. Once the ingots arrived in his factory, the outer skin of bronze was removed from the gold through a heating process, where the lower melting point of the bronze meant that it could be safely stripped away, leaving the gold behind. Then, the shipments would be packaged and sent out to the various interested parties who had placed orders. Many people, he had found, were keen for access to gold that could be easily repurposed as jewellery or simply left in a bank vault as an untraceable chunk of insurance for tough times.

His phone rang in his pocket. He glanced at the screen and answered. "Yes?"

"Mr Castelli. I'm sorry, we ran into a problem in Tunis."

"What sort of problem?" Francesco said. His voice was gentle and mild as if he was speaking to a favourite grandchild who had broken a toy.

"There was a break-in at the warehouse – some thieves were disturbed near the pallets of 60:17 ingots, but nothing was taken."

Francesco frowned. "They definitely didn't take anything?"

"No, sir. Every item is accounted for. We chased the thieves but didn't manage to catch them. They spoke English – sounded British or American." The man sounded relieved that Francesco had taken the news well, and his keenness to let him know how well they'd handled the situation rang through in his voice.

"I see," Francesco said. "Can you describe them?"

"Two men and a woman, all white. The men obviously had some martial arts or combat training. They gave us a run for our money."

Francesco frowned. Was this more than an opportunistic burglary?

Well, there was nothing to be done other than to increase vigilance and security.

"OK. Increase security for the shipments. Keep a careful eye out for any signs that you are under surveillance or being followed," he said.

"Yes, sir," the man replied.

Francesco sat looking at his phone for a long moment after he ended the call, tracing the edges of the ledger on the desk with his forefinger as he thought.

His business – and particularly his new endeavour – had expanded beyond what he had ever dreamed of as a child. The downside of this was the unavoidable need to involve more people and put them in trusted positions. Many criminal organisations fell victim to their own success, he reflected. The need to take on more and more operatives created the opportunity for mistakes or betrayal and made you more conspicuous, both to other criminal groups and to the authorities. He hoped his men in Tunis were telling the truth and hadn't missed anything important in the interaction with the thieves.

Chapter 20 – Palermo to Venice

William smiled as they pulled into the port of Palermo, the ships bobbing cheerfully beneath the towering mass of Monte Pellegrino. The *Accidental Diamond* shone a brilliant white against the bright blue sunny sky.

It was always good to see her. And the dogs. He couldn't wait to feel their heavy, solid heads pushed into his hands as their tails wagged furiously.

Stephen was driving. He looked in the mirror and caught William's eye. "Still asleep?" Stephen asked.

William looked down. Grace had fallen asleep, her head drooping onto his shoulder. She'd slept most of the private jet flight too. "Yep. Tough day all round."

Stephen smiled. "I can't wait to get into my cabin, out of these clothes and into a hot shower. Then a nap before dinner will sort me right out."

"Sounds a sensible idea," William said. Thoughts of a nap, preferably with Grace's soft curves nestled against him as he listened to her breath, were tempting. He shook his head. "But I'll catch up with sleep after dinner. I want to check my emails and see what Amira and Gerrard have come back with ahead of our meeting with them tomorrow."

Stephen pulled the car into the car park.

Grace roused at the stop in motion and stretched. "What a beautiful port!" she said, looking around.

William took a deep breath. The air felt clean, and the cool breeze from the sea, with its hint of salt, was refreshing after the industrial dirt of Tunis and their journey back. His heart skipped a beat as he looked down at her. She had closed her eyes, smiling as she took a deep breath, her face bathed in sunlight. He thought again of her returning to the austere, chilled walls of the prisons.

"Why are you frowning?" Grace asked, her head tilted to one side as she looked at him, a question in her eyes.

He shook his head. "I was thinking of how it does no one any good to be away from the freedom of the sea for too long."

Grace looked out at the sparkling water. "I suppose so. I've lived so long in the city, away from nature, away from the sea, it's easy to forget how good it feels to see open horizons and feel fresh, clean air in our lungs."

"Would you ever move?" William asked casually, leaning against the car as Stephen unloaded their luggage. Stephen's quick eyes darted to him before he looked down, smothering a smile.

Grace hesitated. "Maybe. I often feel constrained in the city, in my job. There isn't a lot of freedom to be yourself." She laughed. "I guess that shouldn't be a surprise, working in the prison system."

"Your counter-corruption and risk assessment skills would be useful in many settings outside the prison sector," William said.

Grace shook her head. "It's such an insular world – I don't know why it's never occurred to me that there are other arenas I could work in."

"Something to think about. We can talk about it when we get this project wrapped up," William replied. He picked up a case and helped Stephen lock up the car before they headed to the *Accidental Diamond*.

Hayley and two other crew members were waiting for them. They assisted them aboard, chatting easily with Stephen and William as they updated them on the sailing conditions and relayed the dogs' antics.

Aurora and Morrigan ran to them as soon as they reached the deck, tails wagging excitedly. Morrigan pushed her head into William's hands, asking for head rubs and ear scratches. Aurora bounded from Stephen to Grace, clearly having decided that it was her job to act as the welcoming committee. William laughed as Aurora leaned her muscular body against Grace's legs, looking up at her lovingly, but almost knocking her off balance with her considerable bulk.

They returned to their cabins and staterooms for a shower and a rest before dinner.

William watched Grace go, the dogs running back and forth, unsure whether to go with her or stay with him. He called them to him, and they flopped down at his feet, but like him, they watched Grace go.

***

The early morning sun shone on the sleek wood on the deck. Even early in the day, the heat was climbing, and Grace welcomed the shade of the canvas awning over them.

William had insisted that they should train before breakfast after checking over her ribs to ensure there was no damage that needed attention. Grace had sat trying to breathe normally as his fingers had probed her bruised ribs, unwilling to show how his touch quickened her heart and left her breathless.

He took chilled bottles of water out of the fridge behind the bar. "I told you I'd be gentle with you." He grinned.

Grace scowled at him. Sweat dampened her hair and her vest clung to her back and breasts. "That was gentle?"

"Yes, we didn't do any floor-work, and I made sure we didn't do anything that would hurt your ribs."

Grace shrugged. "That's true. I guess I'm just not used to it, but if the Tunis situation proves anything, it's that preparation and training are key. I didn't cope well with it."

William pulled a couple of sun loungers under the canopy for them and threw himself into one, long limbs sprawled casually. Grace eased down into the other lounger.

"You're too hard on yourself. You did well. You kept your head, you moved well, you responded to the threats as they came, and you scanned the scene well. Usually, when it's a melee attack, it's messy and unpredictable, and contact is made," he said.

Grace lifted her chin. "I guess so. When I've seen brawls in the prison, it's nothing like in the films, where opponents politely attack one at a time, or in training, where you can perform set pieces. It's usually a scramble of people, arms and legs flailing around as everyone tries to regain control."

"Exactly. Experience helps you keep a situation more under your control, but any conflict of this sort is more of a bar fight than a polished exchange of skills. If you can stay on your feet and keep out of the way of any weapons, that is a pretty good start."

Grace gazed out at the sea. The breeze cooled her damp skin. She found herself dreading the return to London. How had her life shifted so much over such a short time? She thought she'd been happy – or at least not unhappy – dating Dave, living in her flat, working in the prison service. Her work was important to her. She excelled at it, she knew that, and it was satisfying to work on reducing corruption in prisons. But she'd been so focused on her career that she hadn't even thought about what else life could offer. Other places, other people, other opportunities. She sighed. Well, even if she had to go back, maybe this adventure out of her routine would give her the push to look around and make a conscious choice about how she wanted to shape her life. And who she wanted in it.

"That was a big sigh." William's voice jolted her out of her reverie.

"I was thinking about how narrow my horizons have become," she said. "Thank you for giving me the opportunity to broaden them."

William looked at her intently. He seemed about to say something, but with an almost imperceptible shake of his head, instead just said, "It is my pleasure."

Stephen strolled over to them. "Amira and Gerrard will join us on board in an hour."

Grace made to get up and Stephen reached out a hand to pull her to her feet.

"I'll go and shower and meet you at the breakfast table," she said.

Stephen walked with her. "I'll be sorry to see you leave us."

Grace looked at him. "I think I'll be sorry to leave."

"I'm sure there would be opportunities in the Society if you didn't want to leave," he said casually.

Grace shook her head. "I can't imagine that there'd be enough work for a full-time post for me."

Stephen grinned. "Well, I wouldn't rule it out."

Chapter 21 – The Auction

William stood and shook hands with Amira and Gerrard as they joined them at the breakfast table.

They chatted as they ate, catching up on Society news and checking in on how other members were getting on with their endeavours around the world.

As the crew cleared the table, the others moved to the grand salon. Gerrard set up his laptop and connected to the large screen. He displayed a 3-D scan of the ingot.

Amira gestured with the pointer. "With the data you were able to send to us, we have a clear idea about this ingot. The dimensions and relative weight are slightly off what they should be if the ingot were solid bronze. We'd suggest the ingot is, in fact, gold with a thin skin of bronze."

Grace frowned. "How ingenious."

Amira smiled. "Yes, it's quite a nice way of disguising gold for covert transportation. The relative melting points of the metals mean that someone with the correct facilities can melt off the coating without damaging the gold, retaining the bronze for future use and keeping the gold intact to be sold on."

William looked closely at the image. "What are the markings?"

Gerrard rubbed his hands together. "Well, this is how criminals meet their downfall. They can never resist a sly joke. Do you remember the Brinks Mat robberies?"

Grace nodded. "Yes, one of England's biggest gold, jewel and cash heists. A huge amount of the assets were never recovered."

Gerrard flourished his hand in agreement. "Right. To the extent that, if you purchased gold in the United Kingdom after 1983, it probably contains gold from the Brinks Mat robbery. There was limited success in seeking prosecutions, but one of the men convicted had purchased a large house, requiring two large dogs to protect it. Want to have a guess what the dogs were called?"

Stephen snorted. "I think I could take a guess."

Gerrard grinned. "Right. Brinks and Mat."

William laughed. "So what has our villain done here?"

Amira pulled up a new tab on Gerrard's laptop.

"60:17 is a reference to a bible chapter."

Grace read from the screen. "Isaiah 60:17. Instead of bronze, I will bring you gold."

She smiled. "I like this Castelli. He has a sense of humour."

Gerrard nodded. "It's those human quirks that always catch up with criminals in the end."

"What can we piece together of how the Castelli operation functions?" William asked.

Gerrard pulled up a flow chart. "Castelli has worked for years to expand his metals business. Initially, he bought up a small metalworking factory which produced car parts. Since then, he's purchased several factories in the Brescia area and expanded his trading operations, collecting scrap metal from across Europe, shipping it to Africa for processing and receiving reclaimed metals in return."

"That would give him the ideal contacts and foundations to establish a functional smuggling network," said Grace.

"Exactly. His operations have also connected him with crime families and organisations across Europe. When my team started digging, they found that he has extensive contacts with organised crime in every major criminal network in Europe. Scrap-metal trade offers · many opportunities for money laundering, and it seems Mr Castelli has done well in facilitating trade with some very big players," Gerrard continued.

William tapped his fingers on his chin thoughtfully. "And when the Dubai gold-smuggling route collapsed, Castelli must have seen a significant opportunity to innovate and expand his business further."

Amira nodded. "Sarah and I have been tracking the diamond trade. With the information we gained from the Geneva Freeport records, we can see that Castelli has been using diamonds as a means of paying off the gold mines in Africa. He's smart. We think he's getting each crime organisation he's bringing in gold for to send men to attend auctions on his behalf and purchase the diamonds that are sent in payment for the gold. It keeps him off the radar and means there is no one face turning up repeatedly at auctions to raise suspicion."

Grace leaned forward. "What if we set up a diamond auction?"

William raised an eyebrow. "Laying out bait? Yes. That could work."

Gerrard grinned. "I believe someone in the room might have a lure that would work very well."

William rolled his eyes. "You mean the Taylor-Burton?"

Gerrard shrugged, an expression of impish glee on his face.

"It'd certainly catch his attention. And the amount it would sell for would allow for a lot of cash to be cleaned through the trade."

Grace frowned. "The Taylor-Burton? The diamond Richard Burton purchased for Elizabeth Taylor?" She turned to William. "You own Elizabeth Taylor's diamond?"

William spread his hands. "One of them. It was an investment piece, and the proceeds went to build a hospital in Botswana."

Grace sat back in her seat and let out a long breath. "What if we lose it?"

"Worst-case scenario, it'll have been paid for, at least. We can slip a high-tech tracker into the case, and we may get some good data from that," Gerrard said.

"I'll give Jurgen a call to get Interpol on board. There's enough grounds to request that they attend the auction, given our suspicions that high-value diamonds are part of a plan to launder the proceeds of a gold-smuggling operation. We'll take the buyer in for questioning. As soon as he gives enough information – intentionally or otherwise, to justify going after Castelli – Jurgen's men will be ready to raid his offices and bring him in," William said.

"What about the illegal gold mine owners who are being paid in diamonds? Can we bring them down too?" Grace asked.

"We are actively tracking any resale of diamonds matching the description of those we know Castelli has been involved in purchasing," Gerrard replied. "It'll only be a matter of time before we have enough evidence to pass to the authorities on that side, too."

"Amira, can you and Sarah set up an auction of fine jewels and diamonds next week?" William asked.

Amira nodded. "How about the Danieli Hotel in Venice as the auction venue? We have some Society contacts there, and it's an imposing enough location to host the sale of some high-profile items like ours."

"Perfect," William said. "Grace, can you call Jurgen and talk through some potential questions to squeeze the seller with when they bring him in for questioning with Jurgen and his team?" he added.

"Yes, I'll get to it," Grace said.

"Gerrard, Richard is arriving later today. Please liaise with him around surveillance, comms and non-lethal, legal weaponry," said William.

"Non-lethal and legal. Got it," Gerrard said with a disconcerting grin. William narrowed his eyes at him.

"What? That doesn't mean it can't be fun," Gerrard protested.

William looked around the room. "Good work, everyone. It looks like we're close to shutting down another route for illegal gold smuggling. Don't ever forget what that means at ground level. I've seen at first-hand the human and environmental impact of illegal mining."

***

Grace walked down the grand staircase to the main foyer of the Danieli Hotel. It was breath-taking. Sculpted marble wall panels graced with ornate gothic arches framed the stone stairs. The foyer, filled with deep honey-toned carved wood panelling, was furnished with luxurious chairs and elegant tables. Touches of burnished gold glimmered on the stone flowers atop the pillars, and fresh floral arrangements lent elegance and colour to the tables scattered around the room.

Amira and Sarah were waiting for her in the room beside the foyer that they'd reserved for the auction. Chairs were laid out in front of a carved auctioneer's podium, with space for people to stand at the back. Sarah was chatting to the black-suited, white-gloved auctioneer, who, Grace knew, also happened to be a Society member.

Richard opened the door to a side room. He beckoned Amira, Sarah, Grace and the auctioneer to him. In the small, windowless room, Gerrard and William sat at a table. Gerrard had set the room up as a command suite, with surveillance screens and his equipment neatly laid out on a table along one wall. Richard handed each of them a wire kit, consisting of a slender, almost untraceable self-adhesive mic with a matching wireless earpiece that looked like a tiny circular Band-Aid which he'd matched to their skin tone, with instructions on how to fit them. He pulled out a case and unlocked it.

"Right, equipment in case of emergencies – we're limited in Italy: no stun guns or tasers, no firearms, but aerosol self-defence sprays are legal, so that's what we're working with. We have Interpol officers outside the auction room for backup, so this is purely for immediate self-defence whilst you wait for a response from our Interpol friends," he said.

He took a jeweller's loupe, a short magnifying eyepiece set in silver metal, from its case and handed it to Sarah.

"This," he said, "is a high-velocity noxious spray. It also has a powerful light which will dazzle anyone looking at you. If you get into any trouble, point the far end towards the face of your attacker, activate the light by pushing the button and push one end of the loupe towards the other to activate the spray. It has a range of three metres."

"That's very specific," Sarah said, turning the object over in her hands.

"Legal limit for Italy." Richard winked.

"Does it actually work as a loupe?" she said, holding it up cautiously to her eye.

"Yes, it functions like an entirely normal loupe."

"Grace, you have your spray in your thigh holster, right?" Richard asked.

"Right, all in place," Grace replied. The holster fit neatly under her chic pencil skirt without ruining the lines of her suit. The side slit made it easy for her to quickly access the little phial.

"William – this is for you." Richard pulled out an antique silver cigar case.

Richard chuckled. "This one I am rather proud of – it does look beautiful. It will shoot a highly effective, focused spray which will immediately disable an attacker, but the liquid is also infused with UV dyes. Even if we lose our buyer, if we douse them in this, Interpol will be able to identify them later on."

William took it and turned it over in his hands, nodding in approval.

"Oh, I nearly forgot," Richard said, rifling in his jacket pocket. "Here's your lighter."

William looked at him. "To go with my fake cigar case?"

Richard grinned. "Yes. It's a high-powered plasma lighter. It has sufficient charge to give a mild shock at close quarters, which can be useful in taking an attacker's attention off you, but coupled with the cigar case spray liquid, which is flammable, it can also provide a more robust... deterrent."

William smiled and shook his head. "I'm hoping we don't need a flame thrower. It would be rather crass in such lovely surroundings, with so many antiques and delicate, rather flammable-looking, soft furnishings."

"What do I get?" Amira asked.

Richard pulled a pen out of his pocket and presented it to her.

Amira took it, frowning. "A pen?"

"Well, you'll be checking our buyers in, will you not?" Richard said cheerfully.

"Yes, but–"

"And so, you will have the perfect excuse to have this high-spec tactical pen in your hand," Richard continued.

They all looked at it. It was a slim gold pen etched with a Florentine floral motif.

"It is strong enough to break glass. The tip is strong enough to break through flesh and, if applied with sufficient pressure, bone. But obviously, we'd rather not get to that point, if you'll pardon the pun. If you twist the top of the pen anti-clockwise, it will emit an ear-shattering alarm that will distract and disrupt any attempted attacker when held to their ear or thrown at them."

Amira smiled. "Can I keep it?"

Richard winked. "You'll have to ask William nicely."

"And what do you and Gerrard get?" Grace asked.

"Gerrard will be too busy manning the cameras and surveillance equipment, but he has a good old can of pepper spray for backup. And I, as usual, need nothing more than my bare hands," Richard said with a smile.

"And the quick-release weighted belt that doubles as a rope dart, garrotte and restraints?" William added.

"Well, that's just part of my day-to-day aesthetic," Richard replied.

"OK, so we are fully and creatively armed. Thank you, Richard – let's go and fit our wires in the privacy of our rooms and then take up our positions."

***

Grace found her seat in the back row. Amira was greeting people and signing them in at the door. Sarah was standing with the auctioneer. Richard was in the command suite with Gerrard, watching over them. William loitered by the door, directing people to seats and discreetly checking each buyer over. A group of men came in – buyers from Dubai – who William greeted respectfully before seating them.

People drifted in. Men in suits, one or two women, smartly dressed. The seats were almost full, and buyers took standing positions behind the chairs.

"None of the buyers has flagged up on our facial recognition system," Gerrard said through their earpieces.

Grace glanced at William. He gave a tiny shrug. If no one showed up to buy on behalf of Castelli, she was not sure what their next move would be.

"Is this seat taken?" The softly spoken question startled Grace. She glanced up. An attractive woman with long dark hair and striking golden eyes stood beside her. She seemed familiar, Grace thought, searching her brain for where she might have seen the woman. She looked a little like an actress – Salma Hayek, perhaps.

"No, please, help yourself," Grace said, recollecting herself and smiling warmly at the woman.

The woman sat down next to her. "I haven't been here before and was worried about arriving late."

"You haven't missed much. The auction doesn't start for another ten minutes," Grace replied.

"Ah, that is good. I wonder, could I trouble you to show me where the bathrooms are? I arrived in such a rush," the woman said, a note of apology in her voice.

"Of course," Grace said. "They are quite hard to find." She stood up and walked towards the main doors, with the woman following at her heels, intending to point her to the correct niche near the main desk. As they approached the door, Grace felt a prod at her back.

"Keep your eyes to the front and keep walking with me to the bathrooms," the woman said, her voice conver–sational and very quiet. Grace doubted her mic would have picked it up. "I have a slim blade in my hand, and if you make a sound or try to walk away, it will quickly find your spinal cord."

Grace nodded. Her stomach dropped. Now she remembered the face – the woman had been at the restaurant in Palma, the waitress, or so she had seemed. She must be here on behalf of the Majorcan Mafia. And if she recognised Grace, she knew that the auction was a set-up. The question was, was she working alone.

William frowned at her as she passed. Grace smiled and waved a hand towards the bathrooms.

"Where are you going?" Gerrard asked in her ear. "You are all supposed to stay in the main room."

Grace was afraid to reply in case it gave away that she was wearing a mic and earpiece.

She pushed open the bathroom door, the woman close on her heels. Grace whirled as the door shut behind them, reaching for the pepper spray in her thigh holster and kicking out at the woman to try to push her back out of her space. The woman was quick and strong. She blocked Grace's kick in an effortless motion and lunged towards her, pushing her back into the wall and pinning her with a forearm across her throat, the slim blade held tight against her neck with the other hand.

"Are you wearing a wire?" the woman whispered.

Grace didn't reply. The tip of the blade pushed harder into the tender spot under her jawline. Her pulse fluttered against the cold intrusion of the knife. She nodded carefully.

"Remove it," the woman hissed.

Grace pulled the little earpiece from her ear with trembling fingers.

"And the mic?" the woman persisted.

Grace fumbled under her silk blouse and pulled the tiny square free.

The woman took them and, still with one eye on Grace, lifted the lid of a nearby bin and tossed them in. The lid clanged shut. Grace was sure it would mean no one could hear her – she'd lost comms. She swore silently to herself. How had she been so stupid? She should have recognised the woman at once. Those distinctive eyes.

"Well, where do we go from here?" Grace asked, trying to keep her voice even.

"You'll get me out of here," the woman said, "without any fuss. If you do, we part company with no harm done. If I don't leave, then you don't leave."

Grace thought back to her prison training on what to do if you were taken hostage. The first slide had simply said, "Don't make it worse." She'd already broken that rule by trying to fight her way out of the situation – once your adrenaline kicks in, it's hard to keep in mind what you've been taught. What came next? Establish rapport and wait for assistance. It wouldn't be long until someone came to see where she was.

"I remember you," Grace said. "You were at the restaurant with Ramon in Palma."

The woman raised an eyebrow. "I was expecting you to notice immediately. I saw you and the tall man as soon as I entered the auction room. If you had been a little quicker with your recollection, you wouldn't be here now, so I'm thankful for that. Once I had recognised you, I couldn't take the risk of you or the man noticing me and catching me in the trap you'd laid."

Grace inclined her head. "Touché. Are you alone here?"

The woman smiled. "Do you really think I'm going to tell you that?"

Grace shrugged. "I guess not. I was just curious about how you plan to get out of this bathroom. The longer we spend in here, the more likely it is that my team will come looking for me. I don't want this to end in a stand-off. That isn't good for either of us."

The woman looked towards the door. The pressure of the blade against Grace's throat increased, and she struggled not to flinch away from the metal.

"OK, here's what we're going to do. You walk me to the front doors. I watch you walk back inside. You'll wait by the front desk for five minutes. I walk away. No one comes after me," the woman said.

"We better be quick, then," Grace replied.

"Walk in front of me. Don't try anything. My knife is at your back."

Grace turned to the door just as it flew open, kicked hard from the outside. William stormed in, followed by Richard.

The woman grabbed Grace by the throat and pulled her backwards into a cubicle. She shoved Grace into the back of the stall, slamming the door and locking it in a fluid movement.

She turned to face Grace, waving the knife at her. "So, this is the stand-off that isn't good for either of us, right?"

"Right," Grace replied.

"Grace?" William called out to her.

Grace looked at the woman. She waved her knife, gesturing for her to reply. "I'm here," Grace shouted. Her voice came out higher and reedier than she'd intended it to.

"And you, miss – I believe we met briefly in Palma," William said. His calm, clear voice rang out, echoing off the marble tiled walls. "I'm sorry I don't know your name, but I will assume that you are an associate of Ramon's."

"I'm not interested in small talk. Let me walk to the front doors with Grace. I'll go to the bridge with her and leave her there safely if I'm not followed. If I am followed, or if you won't allow me to leave, I'll slit her throat from ear to ear, then slit my own. You won't take me. These are your choices," the woman said, her voice cold and steely.

"I see," William replied. "I thought you might like to know that your companion is now with my team and seems rather willing to talk."

"You're bluffing," the woman called back.

"No, indeed. He has already given up the buyer you are representing, although he's very keen to throw the blame your way. I have to say, he is not nearly as brave as you are." William said. His tone was light and casual. Grace wished she could see his face. Was he worried? She was worried. This woman meant what she said. Grace had a strong sense that she would not shy away from violence and would carry out her threats. She sighed inwardly. Her only choices were to not aggravate the woman and stay calm and focused while William and the team tried to find levers for negotiation.

"Sit," the woman said, pointing.

Grace put the toilet seat down and sat. She clasped her hands between her thighs, trying to subtly use the movement of her legs to shift the phial of pepper spray towards her inner thigh so she could move it into her hands without being seen.

The split in her pencil skirt fell over the top of her left thigh when she was seated. If she worked carefully, she might just be able to get it into her palm without the woman noticing. This, Grace thought, also went against the "don't make it worse" advice, but then she remembered that the final part of that advice was "If you're going to try to escape, be certain that your plan will work. Usually, you're better to wait for assistance." She knew that was true, but what if she could get herself into a situation where she was pretty confident that she could get herself free? Negotiations could end up being long, and that increased the risk of the Majorcan Mafia and Castelli getting wind that something had gone wrong at the auction.

The woman was standing flattened against the side wall of the toilet. The toilets were, unfortunately, well built, each cubicle a little room with solid walls and a solid ceiling, making Grace's escape prospects poor. The woman kept one eye on Grace, her hand still holding the knife towards her throat, and the other on the door, listening for movement and speech outside.

"How about you come out and talk?" William said. "I can assure you that you will not be harmed, and you may be able to secure immunity from conviction in return for information. I can't promise you this, it would be up to Interpol to agree a deal with you, but that's a better prospect than the situation you find yourself in now, isn't it?"

The woman gave a hollow laugh. "I don't trust you, and I don't believe Interpol will cut a deal with me. I prefer my way – you let me get out of this hotel, no one ends up bleeding out on the floor."

"I would also prefer for no one to end up hurt. How about you let Grace go, and I will personally escort you out of the hotel?" William said.

"No. If we do that, all I have is your word of honour that I will leave safely. I learned long ago never to trust anyone's word of honour."

"William," Grace called. "I think we should do as she asks. I will walk with her to the bridge."

The woman looked sideways at her, assessing whether she was being truthful.

There was a long silence. Grace wondered what William was doing, whether he was rapidly forming a plan with the team.

"Alright," he said at last. "I will leave this room. You will walk out of this hotel with Grace, and she will walk with you to the bridge. When you get to the bridge, you may go. We won't go after you as long as Grace is safe and well. If she is harmed in any way, we will come after you like the furies of hell."

The woman looked at the door, assessing William's words. Grace took advantage of her shift in focus to move the fake perfume phial to her palm, using her little finger and the inside of her thumb to wedge it carefully in place.

"Stand," the woman said.

Grace did as she was asked.

"Open the door. Know that my knife is pushed against your back and that any wrong move will result in you regretting that decision, albeit briefly," the woman continued.

Grace nodded. She opened the cubicle door carefully. William was standing to one side by the sinks, hands raised to show that he had no weapons in his hands.

"Stay where you are," the woman commanded as she edged around to open the door, keeping Grace in front of her with an arm on her waist and William in her eye-line at all times. As she turned into the foyer, Grace stumbled forward, breaking the contact of the knife against her back. She fell to her knees on the hard marble floor.

"Up!" the woman said sharply.

Grace put her hands down to raise herself up. As she came to her feet, she spun, pushing back the woman's hands and pushing the phial towards her. The woman clawed at Grace's fingers and she lost her grip, almost dropping her weapon as they struggled, before regaining control and holding the phial close to the woman's face, squeezing the trigger as hard as she could. The liquid came out full force in a wide spray, filling the woman's eyes, nose and mouth.

She dropped the knife as she clasped her eyes and gasped for breath, sagging to her knees, unable to see or draw air into her irritated airways. Grace kicked it away. Gerrard ran forward with Richard, and they grabbed the woman's arms as she struggled to regain her feet. Richard secured her wrists as two Interpol officers dashed forward to take custody of the woman.

Grace stepped away from them. Her heart was pounding and she felt light-headed. William was standing in the doorway of the bathroom, staring at her. The look of warmth and concern in his eyes took her breath away. In a moment, he was with her, folding her against his chest before holding her at arm's length to inspect her throat. Grace lifted her hand to her neck. It felt sore, and when she took her hand away, there was a smear of blood from where the knife had pricked her skin, but she was alive and otherwise unhurt.

William pulled her back into his embrace. "I thought she was going to kill you," he said, his face buried in her hair.

Grace smiled shakily and looked up at him. "So did I. She meant it, you know."

"I know," William said. He reached out and stroked her face.

Grace closed her eyes and felt his lips on hers; passionate, insistent and careless of who was watching, he kissed her. For a long moment, she lost herself in the feel of him, in the relief of being alive.

There was a quiet "Ahem" from behind them.

Grace opened her eyes. A handsome older blonde man stood behind William, wearing an Interpol uniform.

"The man we captured is talking," the officer said. "But we have a problem. He insists that there was a third member of their party, another man."

William frowned. "And where is he?"

The officer spread his hands. "That is the problem. There is no one matching the description the man gave us left in the hotel. Your man is scanning the video footage and will be able to pull up a photo to aid identification, but for now, at least, we have lost him."

William sighed. "Are your men in place near Castelli's offices?"

"Yes, we'll move on him as soon as we can," the officer replied.

"Make it quick. Word will soon get back to the Majorcan Mafia and to Castelli that something went wrong and that they may be compromised," William said.

The officer nodded. "I'll make some calls."

Chapter 22 – Parting

Brescia, Italy, Present Day

Francesco put the receiver down on his desk phone. He lined it up with the jotter and looked out of the office onto the factory floor for a long moment. Someone sang along to a cheerful song on the radio, their fine voice ringing out above the busy sounds from the workbenches.

He smiled. Well, all good things come to an end, and now it was time for a final trade – his wealth for his freedom.

He pulled a set of keys from his pocket and opened the desk drawer. He took out an envelope of papers and placed them on the desk, then slid a small piece of wood across to reveal a tiny keyhole. Francesco unlocked it and then opened an inner compartment. A slim case slid out. Francesco took it, put it into his briefcase and locked the compartment back up.

After a moment's thought, he opened the desk drawer again and, holding the shell to his ear to hear the sea's rush one last time, put it in the empty drawer. It had been his first trade. Only fitting that he should part with it for his last.

Francesco stood, pushed the desk chair neatly back in and walked out of the factory, throwing a wave at the men working at their benches.

As he passed the foreman, he gave him his large bunch of keys. "You're in charge now," he said, handing him the envelope. "The paperwork you'll need is in here. All of this belongs to you and the staff. Run it as a co-operative."

The foreman opened his mouth to speak, but before he could say a word, Francesco patted him on the shoulder fondly and walked on.

Francesco didn't look back as he walked out of the door into the bright, warm sunshine.

***

Jurgen swore softly to himself. It had taken longer than he'd wanted to get a warrant to arrest Castelli and search his premises. He stood staring down at the empty desk for a long moment, then picked up his phone and dialled. "William, it's Jurgen. Castelli has gone. We haven't been able to trace him. There's nothing of note in his office. For some reason, his desk drawer is empty, except for a seashell. Maybe he's letting us know he's gone off to a desert island somewhere, I don't know." Jurgen sighed.

"On the plus side, we have effectively shut down the smuggling route, and Castelli can't hide forever. We'll find him. Thank you for your assistance with this matter. Thanks to you and the Society, there's one less option for the illegal mine owners to profit from their gold. Oh – and one more thing – I just put in my papers for retirement, so I'll be expecting an invite to visit you on the yacht next time you're in my neighbourhood," Jurgen said with a grin.

He chatted for a while with William before saying goodbye, then pressed the end call button and put his phone back in his pocket.

The factory was silent – the staff had been sent home while Interpol and the local police searched the premises. Questioning the staff had yielded nothing. Jurgen looked at the seashell and raised an eyebrow. From what he knew of Castelli, he'd risen from nothing to be a powerful man, then risen from the ashes of personal tragedy to build an empire. Now, he'd left it all behind and gone on the run.

Jurgen might have to hand over the case to his successor if they didn't find him in the next few months. Part of him wished Castelli well. He'd done bad things, but the factory staff's solid refusal to give anything beyond the most basic answers to their questions, not through fear but through loyalty, told him a lot about the man.

Chapter 23 – After the Storm

William put his phone down. He looked across the deck to the table where Amira, Grace, Sarah, Richard, Gerrard and Stephen were all gathered for a post-mission dinner. They were laughing, talking animatedly about the successes and trials of the operation. They were going to be disappointed that Castelli had escaped capture.

He looked at Grace. Her hair was caught up elegantly and pinned back from her face, although a few curls escaped around the nape of her neck. William remembered the feel of her in his arms, the softness of her lips against his, the sharp spike of fear he'd felt when he had thought he might lose her. William clenched his hands hard as he thought about the knife's edge on her vulnerable neck. He would not have been able to bear her loss. It'd been a long time since his heart had ached for someone like this.

He smiled wryly to himself. Perhaps Castelli's escape would give him a reason to keep Grace on his team for a little longer. He could ask her to put together a formulation of potential hypotheses for how he might respond in the current scenario to support Jurgen's team in their investigation. But that would only keep her with him for another week or two at best, and then what? Home to her apartment in the city for her? Back to Shearcourt for him? He didn't relish the prospect. He loved his home dearly, but the thought of being there alone suddenly made him feel cold.

Aurora and Morrigan were curled up at Grace's feet. They would clearly enjoy spending more time with her as much as he would. He was willing to overlook their lack of loyalty, given their clear understanding of Grace's kindness, warmth and sweetness. Her hands traced patterns over their fur as they dozed, content to be close to her.

William took a sip from his glass of whiskey – the same whiskey he'd shared with Grace in Geneva. Their quiet evening in front of the fire seemed so long ago already. It was as if Grace had been in his life for years, not mere weeks. Pushing the thought away, he returned to the table, preparing to tell his team the news that Castelli was now a fugitive.

***

Grace shivered. The *Accidental Diamond* sat at anchor on the Yacht Pier Banchina Adriatica, overlooking Venice. A cool breeze blew over her decks, carrying with it the distant sounds of the city drifting across the water. The faraway lights seemed to wink and shimmer with life, Grace thought as she gazed out. She would miss the peaceful evenings up on deck with William. Grace hated to admit it, but she would miss William. She'd miss the excitement of their mission, the energy of the team, the intrigue of the Society's work – but she'd also miss this quietly strong, capable and generous man.

Gerrard and Stephen had gone to play some war game or other – with Gerrard trying to persuade Stephen of its widespread acclaim for historical accuracy, and the others had gone to their rooms, leaving Grace and William still sitting up on deck beneath the sparkling crystal stars of the canopy. No one had taken the news that Castelli had evaded capture that badly – the success in taking apart the smuggling route was the most important thing, and the intelligence they'd gathered would help ensure that anyone else trying similar methods would have a harder time doing so successfully.

William took off his jacket, draping it over Grace's shoulders.

She looked up at him and smiled. "Thank you. It's getting a little cool out here."

William sat down, turning his chair towards her a little. His legs brushed against hers. Grace rested her knees against his thigh, enjoying the feel of him against her.

He lifted his eyes and held her own in his gaze. "I think you'd find it warmer in my bed," he said softly.

Grace looked back at him. Her eyes were steady, but her cheeks flushed with the warmth that flooded through her and quickened her breath. She nodded.

He drew her gently to her feet and took her hand as they walked below deck.

***

William opened his eyes. Sunshine flooded through the porthole of his stateroom. Grace lay in his arms. His face was pressed against her hair and he breathed her scent in deep. Her hair held the smell of the sea and of summertime. He traced a gentle line down her arm. Her skin was satin smooth beneath his fingertips. She was still breathing the regular, quiet pattern of sleep. His body stirred at the memory of her the night before, of the taste and feel of her. She shifted in his arms and opened her eyes. A lazy smile lit her face as she put her hand in his and nestled into him.

"Good morning," she said, her voice husky and sweet.

"It is a good morning," he replied with a grin.

She laughed softly. He smoothed her hair and rolled onto his back, making space for her to snuggle under his arm. She turned and laid her head on his shoulder, an arm draped over his chest.

"I have been thinking," he began. She lifted her head to look at him curiously. "I wondered whether you might consider joining the Society more permanently."

174

She frowned. "Were you wondering this before we slept together?"

William paused. "Yes, my feelings for you and my thoughts about your role in the Society are two different things."

Grace raised an eyebrow. "But that is rather a problem, isn't it?"

William frowned. "Why is it a problem?"

Grace pushed herself up and sat looking down at him. "Because if we have feelings for one another, then we shouldn't be working together, and besides, who would be my boss if I were to join the Society?"

Her voice was crisp and cold, businesslike and aloof. He'd messed this up.

"Well, technically, I would be, but–" he began.

"There is no but, William. You can have me as a romantic partner, or you can have me as an employee. You can't have me as both." Grace stood up and began gathering her clothes.

"I want you as an equal partner, Grace. In both parts of my life," William said. His heart ached as she moved around the room, refusing to meet his eye.

"I need some time to think," she said as she pulled on her dress.

Chapter 24 – A Gift

Grace pulled off her boots and sat down in front of the fire. The house in Geneva felt strange without William. She was glad that Amira and Sarah had been able to join her for a break. It took her mind off his absence.

"All of that fresh air has made me hungry!" Amira smiled at the chef, who appeared from the kitchen, carrying a tray of hot chocolate and snacks.

"The forests around Yannick's estate made for a beautiful ride," Sarah said, helping herself to a cookie.

Grace sipped her hot chocolate. "This is delicious, but I feel it needs a little something to boost its restorative powers."

She went over to explore the bottles arranged on the bookcases, examining each in turn before settling on a bottle of rum. There was a bureau in the centre of the long row of shelves. Grace opened the drop-down cabinet at the centre, searching for a spirit measure. Her hand froze with the cabinet half-open. The warm, cheerful light of the living room shone on a photo album. The cover had a photo of William. He stood outside a chalet in the snow with Stephen and a woman. A beautiful young woman with long blonde hair. A knot tightened in her stomach. She let the cabinet open fully.

"Grace?" Amira was looking at her as if she'd asked her a question.

"Sorry." Grace shook herself. "I got distracted."

Amira came over and looked over Grace's shoulder. She took out the photo album.

"Ah. I see. This is what distracted you?"

Grace nodded.

Amira took her hand and steered her back to the sofa, bringing the bottle of rum with them. She poured a generous measure into each of their hot chocolates. Sarah fetched blankets from the basket by the fire.

Amira opened the album on her lap between them.

"This–" she pointed to a photo of the same young woman, this time in a cap and gown "–is Sadie."

"You probably haven't heard William talk much about her, if at all. He doesn't like to boast," Sarah added.

"Boast?" Grace frowned.

"He and Stephen are very proud of her," Amira said, turning the page. There was a photo of Stephen holding the reins of a pony, a little blonde girl of perhaps eleven or twelve sitting proudly on its back.

"I'm lost. Is this William's daughter? He's never mentioned having any children."

"No, not exactly," Sarah said.

"Did William ever tell you about his time in Afghanistan?" Amira asked.

"No, I know he's seen active service and that he, my governor at the prison and Stephen served together, but not much more than that," Grace said.

Amira turned a couple of pages in the album, searching the photos. She tapped a page. "This–" she indicated to a photo of a young-looking William sitting with a handsome blonde man "–was Sadie's father, Henri. He was a French doctor working for the Red Cross in Afghanistan. William and Stephen got to know him well."

Grace examined the photo. Henri had a kind, open face and a wide, genuine smile. "I see. They were friends?"

Sarah sighed. "Yes, they were. Henri was killed by an IED that also injured William. Stephen was unhurt and pulled them both to safety, but Henri couldn't be saved."

Grace put her hand to her mouth as she looked down at the photo. She'd worked with many ex-servicemen over the years. Stories like this were all too familiar – she knew the damage that a trauma like that could leave across many lives.

"How old was Sadie when it happened?"

"Ten years old," Amira replied. "William went to see Henri's wife, Claudia, as soon as he recovered from his injuries. They were close for several years, but Claudia was sadly killed in a car accident over ten years ago."

"Did you know her?" Grace's heart squeezed painfully. So much loss.

"Yes, we all did. She was a lovely person," said Sarah.

"What happened to Sadie after her mother died?"

Amira smiled and flipped the album pages until she found a photo of William, Stephen and Sadie in front of a Christmas tree, a pile of half-opened presents around them.

"William and Stephen did their best to make a home for Sadie in Ireland. William supported her to finish school in Geneva and then to study for a degree in Politics and International Studies at Cambridge."

"How old is she now?" Grace took the album, fascinated, and turned the pages.

"Twenty-four." Sarah smiled. "And newly recruited to MI6, not that we're supposed to know. She's just moved to Vienna."

"I think William and Stephen miss having her around at Shearcourt Demesne," Amira added.

"Huh." Grace sat back on the sofa and sipped her hot chocolate. The warmth of the rum helped undo the cold tightness in her stomach. "He really is a difficult man to get to know."

Sarah shrugged. "Perhaps. William doesn't give a lot away. He doesn't like to talk about his accomplishments or the good things he does for others, but he is a very loyal, principled man. That's clear in his actions, even if he doesn't say a lot."

"Oh, I know that," Grace agreed.

There was a knock at the door. Grace looked around. Chef was busy in the kitchen.

"I'll get it," she called as she ran to the porch.

"Delivery for you, Madam," a young courier said politely, holding out a beautifully wrapped box.

"Thank you." Grace signed the sheet he handed her and took the package, closing the door.

"What's that?" Sarah said, her face alive with curiosity.

"I don't know – a package. There isn't a name on it." Grace turned the box in her hands, looking for a card.

"From William, I suppose," Amira suggested, taking the box from her.

"Let's open it." Sarah took it from Grace and walked to the dining table to set it down.

Grace fetched a letter opener, and they slid off the ribbon and sliced through the seals on the edges of the box.

"Ah, Läderach." Amira pointed to the gold lettering on the inner box. "He sent us chocolate. How kind."

Grace took the lid off. Inside, nestled in golden paper, were exquisite chocolate seashells, each one a different design, delicately picked out.

"Oh, look at these, how beautiful!" Grace breathed.

"I'll call him to say thank you." Amira dialled William's number and put her phone on speaker.

"Good evening, Amira." William's voice came from the speaker. Grace felt a stab of longing at his familiar tones.

"I'm here with Sarah and Grace. We just wanted to say thank you for the beautiful chocolates."

There was a long pause.

"What chocolates?"

Amira raised an eyebrow. "The seashells, from Läderach. The courier just delivered them."

"Put them down and don't eat any," William said sharply.

Grace dropped the box on the table in surprise.

"Where's Chef?"

"In the kitchen." The three women looked at each other, concern on their faces.

"Please call him."

The chef had already joined them, hearing the change in their voices.

"I'm here, sir."

"You need to take Grace, Amira and Sarah to the chalet at Crans-Montana, Jacob. I'll call Stephen and Gerrard and brief them about the situation. We'll pull the CCTV to look at the courier. Leave the chocolates on the table. I'll have someone pick them up for analysis. Everyone who touched the box, wash your hands and don't touch the package or wrapping again."

"Yes, sir."

"Grace, Amira, Sarah – I am concerned that this is a breach of security and potentially an attack. We'll reconvene for further discussion when you arrive. The house is secure, private and well-protected."

"Understood, we'll start packing." Amira lowered the phone to end the call.

"Wait, Amira! Did you say seashells?"

***

Grace stood on the balcony of the chalet. The bright blue sky, white snow and deep green forests were dazzling. The intensity of the colours reminded her of an old-fashioned technicolour picture postcard. The crisp mountain air held the scent of pine and wood smoke.

It would be charming if she wasn't worried about security breaches and a possible poisoning attempt. She laughed softly to herself for trying to pretend that she wasn't enjoying the intrigue and excitement. She'd be back in London next week if they got the all-clear. Back to work. Back to her apartment. Back to her life.

Sarah joined her on the balcony. "Conference call in fifteen minutes. Gerrard has updates."

"Great, is Amira still on the phone with the lab?"

"Yes, she should be free to join us by then."

They arranged chairs in front of the large TV.

William's and Gerrard's faces filled the screen.

Amira slid into a chair, a notepad in her hand.

"Good to see you all. Amira, do you want to give your update first?" William asked.

She flipped her notepad open. "The lab has conducted a thorough analysis of the package. There are no indications that the chocolates were tampered with in any way. The only fingerprints are those of the courier and the shop staff."

Grace raised an eyebrow. "So someone just wanted to send us a calling card?"

"Yes, Mr Castelli, it seems. The only item left in his desk when Interpol raided his office was a seashell. Jurgen hasn't been able to make any sense of it, but it seems like this was a little nod from Mr Castelli, just to let us know that he knows who we are."

"Are there any leads in the search for him?" Sarah asked.

"Nothing." Gerrard rubbed his hands over his face. "Interpol has nothing, and we've had no luck making any connections with the chocolates. They were paid for in cash, there's no CCTV in the shop or street, and the shop staff couldn't recall much about the man who paid for the delivery."

"What does this mean from a security perspective?" Grace had brief visions of them being forced to move from chalet to beach house to… wherever else William or the Moonlight Society had places until Castelli was caught. It wasn't the worst thing she could imagine.

"It seems clear that he didn't intend harm." William shrugged.

"But we've got good security coverage in London, Grace, so we'll ensure you are safe. Amira and Sarah –

Gerrard and Richard will review your existing security arrangements with you."

Grace nodded. "And are we safe to stay here for the rest of the week?"

"Jacob will accompany you on any trips out. The security in the house is good, and we have additional support nearby if needed, so I'd suggest you enjoy the snow for a few days more." William smiled.

Chapter 25 – You Can't Go Home Again

Grace lay on her sofa, restless and irritable, her work laptop open in front of her as she waded through the backlog of emails. Her apartment, with its background hum of traffic, felt like a cage in the warm late-spring sunshine. Grace looked out of the window. It was the weekend. She should go out and walk in the park or something. She looked back at the unread emails. But then she'd be thinking of her inbox and the presentation she needed to finish by Monday for submission to a major international anti-corruption conference in Milan.

Returning to work had, at least, offered a distraction from her thoughts. At the back of her mind was a restless dissatisfaction with her life. Her work felt repetitive, and there were endless meetings which rarely resulted in action. She missed the freedom and fresh ocean air on the *Accidental Diamond*. She missed the team. She missed their camaraderie and a shared mission. And most of all, though she hated to admit it, she missed William.

Despite the drama, the week in Switzerland, with long days walking in the mountains and forests, riding at Yannick's and eating lazy lunches by the water, had been pleasant. But all the time, the prospect of returning home had sat heavily on Grace's heart. She felt guilty. She'd worked hard to get to where she had in her career. She had a home, a good job, and friends and a family in London. Many people envied her job and were striving to get to the level she'd achieved. It was ungrateful to feel dissatisfied.

Her phone buzzed. She looked down. An incoming call from Dave. She rolled her eyes and pressed the side button of her phone to silence the call. The screen stayed lit with Dave's name and photo for a long moment before he gave up and the light dimmed. Grace sighed. She should be grateful for Dave, too. He was a nice man.

But he wasn't William Anderson. Grace's mind snagged on the memories of him – the sound of his deep, melodic voice, his assured touch, gallant manners, generous spirit and loyal heart. Despite his refinement, the man moved like a panther, filled with an understated but unmistakable power. She had never met a man like him, and he refused to leave her thoughts.

Grace flicked on her TV, annoyed with herself. The news station showed the haul of bronze-coated gold ingots recovered from the Castelli shipments. The segment hailed the success of the Interpol operation, in collaboration with several police forces across Europe, in bringing down the smuggling ring. Grace smiled. It felt good to know she'd had a part to play in that. She shook her head at the piece of her that already wanted to know what the next operation would be.

She and William had parted, carefully polite, regretful, with a promise to talk soon. But Grace did not know what to say. How could she choose? If she decided to pursue a relationship with William, she couldn't maintain her career in the prison service and see him with any sort of regularity over the long term. If she chose to become a member of the Moonlight Society, she couldn't be William's lover. She didn't want her life to remain as it was, but maybe it was just easier that way.

Her heart squeezed painfully at the thought of not seeing William again. She gritted her teeth. Well, one thing she could do was keep up with her self-defence training. That would be a good distraction. She typed "krav maga" and her area into the search bar on her phone and scrolled through the results.

A dojo near her offered classes on Monday evenings – she'd book to go along for a trial class. Grace wanted to keep building on the skills she'd learned with Stephen, and – here, she carefully steeled her thoughts against the memories of their training sessions – with William.

***

William sat in a handsome leather wingback chair at his desk, looking out of the tall sash windows across the gardens of Shearcourt Demesne. Stephen was walking across the lawns on his way to the stables, Aurora and Morrigan running at his heels.

The sun lit the fresh green of the fields and sparkled on the water. Grace would love the house, he thought. She'd enjoy the wildness of the Atlantic Coast weather, the lushness of the countryside and the liveliness of the horses, dogs and farm animals. Where would she be now? he wondered. In her apartment, out eating brunch with her mother, or perhaps, on a date? William tapped his fingers on his desk, impatient with himself. Since he'd returned home, everything around him, he'd seen with an earnest desire to show it to Grace, to see her face light up with pleasure and interest.

He couldn't shake her hold on his heart. Nor, if he was honest, did he want to. But how to resolve the impasse they found themselves at? William admired her integrity – how could he find a way for them to build a relationship whilst offering her the opportunity to further her career? She had the expertise the Society needed, regardless of what William thought or felt about her. She had worked well with the team, shown flexibility and creative thinking and brought experience that would benefit a wide range of operations the Society engaged in.

William shook himself. He had been so lost in thought that he had lost track of time and had sat too long at his desk. William stretched, feeling chilled and stiff. This morning, he had lit the double-sided stove, which heated the large, welcoming kitchen and the study. Despite the sunshine, there was a bite to the air, and, truth be told, he liked the comfort of the ritual of laying the fire. He'd laid the seasoned wood and blocks of turf, adding kindling and tending it until a bright blaze shone in the grate. The cheerful crackle, left untended once William had become absorbed in his work, had begun to die down. He glanced down at the stove. Only smouldering embers remained, pulsing with heat and light.

William frowned as he gazed out of the window. Clouds scudded across a bright blue sky. He stood – perhaps some fresh air would do him good. He'd follow Stephen down to the stables to see how the horses were coming on.

He pulled a dark green wax jacket from a hook near the door and pushed his feet into a pair of worn riding boots waiting by the French windows.

William walked down to the stables, looking up when the high keening sound of a buzzard caught his ear. Out on the grass, the wind raked its wild fingers through his hair, the salt scent of the sea sharpening the air with its tang. The dogs, hearing his steps, came running to greet him, tails high in the air and wagging vigorously. William smiled and administered head pats and ear rubs to them both before walking over to join Stephen in the tack room.

Stephen was thoroughly brushing Flexalan leather dressing into the worn straps of a bridle hung from a hook on the tack room wall.

"Morning, Stephen," William said. He took another bridle, inspected it before hanging it, and took a damp sponge from a selection Stephen had set out on the table. William rubbed it in a jar of saddle soap and began to work his way over the leather.

Stephen waved a hand in greeting.

They worked in companionable silence. William breathed in the smell of the tack room – he loved the scent of horses and leather. It made him feel at home. He and Stephen had worked side by side like this many times over the years. He smiled, thinking of their cavalry days when keeping their uniforms, their horses and their saddlery immaculate had taken up much of their time. He missed the simplicity of those days.

"How's Grace?" Stephen asked.

William gave a wry smile. He could count on Stephen not to beat around the bush.

"I haven't spoken to her."

"Why not?" Stephen said, still working vigorously at the bridle, polishing the metal fittings with a soft cloth.

William sucked in a breath before replying, weighing his words carefully. "I don't know what to say," he said simply.

"Explaining how you feel might be a good start. Call me old-fashioned," Stephen said.

And he'd decided he'd come down to the stables to get away from his thoughts about Grace. "I think she knows. But there are practicalities that I haven't worked out how to solve. Yet." He passed the clean leather through his fingers, inspecting the stitching.

"Well, best get on with it," said Stephen. "She might not still be available if you take too long coming up with a suggestion."

"No, no, please don't hold back, Stephen," William said with a wry grin. "And if you have a solution in mind, I'm all ears."

"Gerrard," Stephen said.

"Gerrard?" William replied, puzzled.

"Yep. He's an independent contractor, right?"

"Right."

"And so, he doesn't work for you but still works for the Society and is a Society member?" Stephen continued.

"Yes," William said thoughtfully.

"So why wouldn't that work for Grace? She'd have the chance to do something that stretched her and gave her freedom if she set up independently. The contracts from the Society would be a good start and would provide enough for her to live on initially, but she'd have the autonomy to grow her business as she likes," Stephen said.

"Why do I feel you've given some thought to this?" William said suspiciously.

"Well, we felt like you were dragging your heels." Stephen shrugged.

"We?" William said.

"Me, Amira, Gerrard, Sarah, Richard…"

"I see." William smiled warmly.

"And did you, as my group of unsolicited advisors, come up with a plan of how to communicate this to Grace?" he added.

"We thought that'd be best coming from you, but Amira and Sarah will send you a draft business plan for her, Gerrard has offered to mentor her through her first year in business, and Richard offered his services to design logos and branding for her and to build her website," Stephen said briskly.

William shook his head, smiling. To his surprise, he felt a lump in his throat. His team had seen his dilemma, seen Grace's worth and importance to the team, and come up with not just a solution but a real opportunity that would offer her everything he felt sure she wanted. Travel, adventure, challenges that would stimulate her mind and allow her to use her considerable skills and, most importantly, the opportunity to build a foundation for herself that offered her total independence and flexibility. The freely offered agreement and support of the team would make it clear to her that this was not a proposal that came from him alone but from the Society and the people she had worked hard to build relationships with. William pushed down the thoughts about how his own future with Grace might emerge. Grace needed space to consider the opportunity on her own terms.

"You'll be wanting to go to London within the next few days, I'd guess," Stephen said.

William nodded. "Yes, please arrange me a flight."

Epilogue

Francesco sat in the dimly lit living room of a small London flat. It was on the fourteenth floor of a grim, grey tower block and the bright spring day seemed far away in the city's press. His muscles ached, and his skin felt dull and lifeless without the sunshine of home.

The cheap tracksuit he'd picked up when he'd arrived felt baggy and ungainly. He felt untidy, and it made him uneasy. Francesco missed the crisp feel of his fine shirts and bespoke suits. How, he thought, could people conduct their day-to-day business wearing clothes that were like particularly poor-quality pyjamas?

He held the keys to the flat in his hands. They'd been pushed under the grimy doormat, as he'd been told they would be. There was no keyfob, just a Yale lock and deadlock key for the front door on a plain metal ring. He turned the ring between his fingers, letting the keys dangle gently, jangling against one another with a metallic sound.

His phone rang. He answered it on the second ring.

"Yes?" he said.

"Francesco, good to speak to you. I have reviewed your request, and I think we can reach a mutually beneficial agreement." The voice on the other end of the phone was gruff and direct.

"I'm pleased to hear it." Francesco spoke English well – he'd done enough business around Europe to find it helpful to acquire a solid understanding of the language over the years.

"Unfortunately, we recently lost an Italian jeweller who had been working with us for a long time," the man continued.

Lost, thought Francesco. Killed was the more honest translation. He shrugged. It was no business of his what had happened to the man.

"Now, we happen to have his documents and – as you can see – access to his residence."

Francesco looked around. A gaudy Virgin Mary statuette formed the base of a lamp on the bookcase. It sat alongside a neatly folded set of reading glasses, placed on top of a half-finished crossword puzzle on the coffee table, the pen still waiting to be picked back up. There was little enough in this sad flat to show for a life.

"The police are looking for our gentleman due to an outstanding warrant for breach of licence conditions, causing us some concerns. It would be inconvenient for the police to ask too many questions at this time," the man said conversationally.

"How long was he due to go back in for?" Francesco asked.

"Twelve months."

Francesco nodded to himself. Yes, that would work well. No one would be looking for a fugitive criminal in prison, and after twelve months, his new identity would be well cemented, and the hunt for Francesco Castelli would have died down.

"Hand yourself in at Forest Gate Police station tomorrow morning. There's a folder with ID and court papers so you can familiarise yourself with your new history in the bottom drawer of the TV cabinet," the man said.

"OK, we have a deal," Francesco said.

***

William looked around fondly at Magee's drapery shop. He had his first suit made here, as did his father and grandfather. The little shop he had known had expanded into a more refined store over the years, but it still held an old-fashioned charm, from the books of fabric swatches, tweeds and wools made at local mills around Donegal to the polished wooden display cases.

William stood in the fitting room. The tailor worked away with his tape, jotting down measurements as he went. William would fly to London tomorrow morning to meet with Grace.

He bit his lip – what if she rejected his proposal?

Amira and Sarah's business plan had arrived printed and neatly bound, with a slick brochure of draft logos and website mock-ups from Richard and a letter from Gerrard soon after his conversation with Stephen.

He really needed to think about Stephen's role in the Society and his potential for development. He had steadfastly refused promotion, insisting that he preferred to remain working closely with William and developing the horses. Perhaps Stephen would consider taking a lead role in their equestrian businesses. It was his passion and would give him more time to build some roots and a life for himself.

The tailor finished taking his measurements and was noting them down with William's choices of fabric, lining and detailing when William's phone vibrated from his jacket pocket.

He pulled it out and glanced at the screen. Smiling apologetically at the tailor, he excused himself and stepped outside to take the call.

"William? It's Ian."

"Ian! How are you? I got Grace back to you on time – early in fact, and in one piece, as agreed," William said cheerfully.

There was a long pause at the other end of the phone.

"Yes, thank you," Ian said, his flat tone at odds with his words.

William waited, a chill rising in his stomach and a frown settling on his face.

"What's wrong?" he said after a long moment listening to Ian's uneven breathing at the other end of the phone.

"Thomas Campbell is dead," Ian said at last.

William sucked in a breath.

Thomas had been a fellow cavalryman in their regiment, best man at Ian's wedding and one of William's closest friends. He leaned against the shop doorway. All of the air seemed to have left his lungs.

"What happened?"

Ian was silent, and William found himself again listening to the faraway thread of his breath, in and out, in and out.

"He was shot once in the head, at long range, while he was out in the fields on the farm," Ian said. His voice was hoarse and uneven.

William swore softly under his breath, his fingers gripping his phone so hard that the knuckles whitened.

"I'll be in London tomorrow," he said. "We'll talk then."

"Come to the house," Ian said. "Shona wants to see you."

Tears pricked William's eyes.

Shona, Ian's fierce, kind, brilliant wife, must be desperately upset. Thomas and his family had been part of Ian's own family. Their children were friends.

And God, Thomas's wife. What a mess.

"Of course. See you tomorrow," he said.

William ended the call and stood in the doorway, fighting the nausea that threatened to choke him.

A single shot to the head at long range. That was a professional job.

How had Thomas made enemies powerful enough to warrant an assassination?

William took a deep breath.

Well, it looked like he would need Grace sooner rather than later. He needed her skills. He needed her objectivity, because he was too close to this situation.

But there was no question that he could allow the police to investigate without the assistance of the Moonlight Society. He owed it to Thomas, his family, and their friends to find out what had happened.

He only hoped that the threads he'd have to unravel wouldn't pull apart the tapestry of Thomas's life.

The End